REX ZERO

KING OF NOTHING

ALSO BY TIM WYNNE-JONES

STORIES

Lord of the Fries and Other Stories

The Book of Changes: Stories

Some of the Kinder Planets

NOVELS

Rex Zero and the End of the World

A Thief in the House of Memory

The Boy in the Burning House

Stephen Fair

The Maestro

KING OF NOTHING

TIM WYNNE-JONES

MELANIE KROUPA BOOKS

FARRAR, STRAUS AND GIROUX · NEW YORK

Copyright © 2008 by Tim Wynne-Jones
First published by Groundwood Books Limited, Canada
First American edition, 2008
Printed in the United States of America
Designed by Irene Metaxatos
10   9   8   7   6   5   4   3   2   1

www.fsgkidsbooks.com

Library of Congress Cataloging-in-Publication Data
Wynne-Jones, Tim.
    Rex Zero, king of nothing / by Tim Wynne-Jones.— 1st ed.
        p.   cm.
    Summary: In 1962 Ottawa, eleven-year-old Rex Norton-Norton faces
several confusing mysteries, including his father's troubling secrets
from World War II, the problems of a beautiful but unhappy woman
named Natasha, what to do about his mean and vindictive teacher,
and whether or not he should even be concerned about these things.
    ISBN-13: 978-0-374-36259-1
    ISBN-10: 0-374-36259-9
    [1. Coming of age—Fiction.   2. Family life—Canada—Fiction.
3. Interpersonal relations—Fiction.   4. Schools—Fiction.
5. Ottawa (Ont.)—History—20th century—Fiction.   6. Canada—
History—1945—Fiction.]   I. Title.

PZ7.W993 Rey 2008
[Fic]—dc22
                                                        2007008181

THIS BOOK IS FOR DAD
1912–1981
AND FOR ALL THE OTHER SOLDIERS
AND WHAT THEY CARRY

REX ZERO

KING OF NOTHING

OUR MISTRESS DAY

I t always rains on Our Mistress Day. That's what I'm hoping for tomorrow, freezing November rain as sharp as vaccine needles. The kind of rain my mother would never let me go out in.

"It's called Remembrance Day," says James.

"Except in the States," says Buster. "They call it Veterinarians Day."

"Veterans Day," says Kathy, rolling her eyes.

Buster laughs as if he was fooling. You can never tell with Buster.

"Well, my dad calls it Our Mistress Day," I tell them. "I don't know why. But I hope it rains even worse than this. I hope it pours."

It's Saturday, November 10, 1962, and the four of us are watching the protesters on Parliament Hill in Ottawa. The rain has made their BAN THE BOMB signs bleed. They're waiting for Prime Minister Diefenbaker to show his face. Canada doesn't have any bombs, I don't think—not like the U.S.A. and Russia. Last month they had a fight about Cuba and almost started World War III. I'm not sure Diefenbaker can do much to stop them, but the protesters seem to think he can.

"Where's Dief the Chief!" they shout. "Where's Dief the Chief!"

"Yeah, where *is* Dief the Chief?" says Kathy impatiently.

"Ah, he's not going to show," says Buster.

"He'd better," says Kathy. "I've got a thing or two to tell him." And she will, if she gets the chance. She's very brave. Like her dad, a pilot who got killed in the Korean War.

"Where's Dief the Chief!" shouts Kathy. "Where's Dief the Chief!"

"I think Buster's right," says James. "The prime minister's probably sitting in front of his fireplace listening to the game on the radio."

"Holy moly!"

I totally forgot. The Ottawa Rough Riders are playing the Montreal Alouettes in the Eastern Conference quarterfinals.

I look at James's watch. I have to rub away the beads of rain on the crystal. Two o'clock. Kickoff time.

"Diefenbaker is from Saskatchewan," says James, "so he's probably hoping Ottawa loses."

"Why?" says Kathy.

"Because of the Saskatchewan Roughriders."

"There are two teams called the Rough Riders?" Kathy knows lots of things but football isn't one of them. "Isn't that confusing?" she asks.

"The Saskatchewan Roughriders are out west," says Buster. "In Saskatchewan."

"And they're spelled differently," says James. "The Saskatchewan team is just one word, Roughriders."

"Yeah, but what if both teams made it to the Grey Cup and you were listening to it on the radio, so you couldn't tell who was who," I say.

"The Rough Riders are passing," I say in my best broadcaster's voice. "Oh, no! The Roughriders have intercepted! Look, the Roughriders are trying to block the Rough Riders who are trying to tackle the Roughriders. Hooray, they've scored. The Roughriders have scored!"

Everybody laughs. Then suddenly Kathy is grabbing my arm, jumping up and down, and pointing to the line of protesters.

"In the red tam with the yellow pom-pom. See? See? Isn't that Miss Cinnamon?"

It is. Our sixth grade teacher—the best teacher ever. Except she left, about two weeks ago, because she's expecting a baby.

"I still don't get how she can be *Miss* Cinnamon if she's having a baby," says Buster.

"Because she isn't married," says Kathy. "You don't have to be married to have a baby."

"That's the part I don't get," says Buster.

"Well, Kathy's mom is a nurse, so she'd know," says James.

And Buster and I both agree.

Just then Miss Cinnamon sees us and waves. We all wave back. She's hanging on to the arm of a tall man with a beard. He waves, too.

"I guess their sign says it all," says Kathy.

"BAN THE BOMB! SAVE THE WORLD FOR OUR CHILDREN," reads the sign in the tall man's hands.

"Yeah," says James to Kathy and me. "But who's going to save *you*?" He and Buster are in Mr. Gallup's class. Kathy and I are stuck with the replacement teacher from hell, Miss Garr.

I look at Kathy, still waving. Then she drops her hand and her shoulders sag. Miss Garr is pretty scary, all right. My dad told me a gar is a kind of fish with a long snout and lots of teeth. Some people call them needlefish. Well, that's Miss Garr. She likes to needle people.

I pat Kathy on the shoulder. She shakes me off.

"It's cold," she says. "Let's go."

We're all shivering. Home begins to seem like a really good idea. I leap on my trusty Raleigh three-speed, and we peel out of there so fast the protesters' shouts are soon just a distant murmur.

The rain isn't hard but it's steady, and you have to squint when you get into high gear. Hey, maybe I'll catch pneumonia! Then it won't even matter if the weather is horrible tomorrow. They can't make me go if I'm in the hospital. I swerve to hit a puddle.

It isn't fair. I have three older sisters, as well as a younger sister and brother, but I'm the only one in the family who has to go with Dad to the War Memorial tomorrow for the Our Mistress Day service.

"There'll be real soldiers with guns," says Buster.

"There'll be marching bands with three hundred thousand bagpipers," says James.

"You should feel proud," says Kathy.

"I am proud," I say, but I don't sound it. "It's going to be so boring. I just know it." They all agree. What I really want to say is that I'm scared, scared of letting my father down. But I can't tell them that. And I can't tell them why.

I make it home in time for the second quarter of the game, but Mum won't let me listen to the radio until I change into pajamas. Then I sit in the living room with Dad in front of *our* fireplace with a blanket around me and my feet in a tub of hot water, drinking barley soup from a mug and listening to *our* Rough Riders lose.

"You could have caught your death of cold," Mum says, tucking me in.

"Good," I mutter. "Then I won't have to go to the memorial service." I say this under my breath, but not far enough under my breath.

"What was that?" says Dad. His eyebrows are all

bunched together into one huge, hairy eyebrow, and every hair looks angry.

"Nothing."

He looks toward the ceiling. "Must be those pesky little no-see-ums. I could have sworn I heard a teensy insectlike voice complaining about something."

I look for no-see-ums until I think he's stopped glaring at me. I check. He's looking into the fire. I don't think he's listening to the game. I can hardly hear it myself. All I can think about is tomorrow.

"Our Mistress Day."

"What did you say?"

I didn't realize I had said it out loud. "Our Mistress Day."

"It's *Armistice* Day," says Dad, spelling it out. "Good grief, Rex."

"Armistice? What's that?"

"Truce," says my father. "The end of the war." He puffs away at his pipe. "It comes from the old Swahili word meaning no more lumpy porridge."

I'll never understand how my father can be funny when he's in a foul mood, and he *is* in a foul mood, that's for sure.

"The Americans call it Veterans Day," I tell him.

"Trust the Yanks," says my father. "They didn't even join the bloody war until they'd finished bloody dessert. The Brits and the Canadians had been slogging through the mud since bloody breakfast."

It's a three-bloody sentence, which means he is really riled.

It's halftime in the football game and we're sitting there in the living room, just the two of us, silent now. I don't know what to say. Nothing? That seems like a good idea. Then Mum comes in with more soup for me and another corned beef and Branston pickle sandwich for Dad. There is a furrow in his forehead you could park a Pontiac in.

"Our Mistress Day," he says again. "Did you hear that, Doris?"

Mum is tucking my blanket around me. She looks as if she has her own foul mood she's working on and doesn't want to be interrupted.

"Do you think war is some kind of blooming love affair, Rex?" says Dad.

I've seen the documentaries on TV. I've seen the shrapnel wounds in my father's knee. I know war isn't any fun, which is why we should just get over it, shouldn't we?

"The war ended in 1945, right?" I say. "That's seventeen years ago. Why should we keep remembering all that horrible gunky stuff?" Especially if you have to remember it standing in the pouring rain in scratchy flannel pants, I want to add. But from the expression on Dad's face, I think I'd better shut up. He looks as if he is going to raise his voice, but then he snaps his mouth shut and just fills his pipe instead. His eyes are full of something, though.

A storm. Bigger than the one outside.

SUNDAY

rmistice Day and the sun is shining! It's cold in my room at the top of the house but not cold enough to catch your death.

"I'm really worried about going to the service with Dad tomorrow," I said to Mum the night before, when she came to tuck me in.

"It's important for your father, Rex."

"Then why is he so crabby?"

"He always gets that way around now."

How can I explain to Dad that even though I've been practicing and practicing I'm not ready?

You see, I'm afraid I'll faint.

I'm *sure* I'll faint.

I climb out of bed and shiver until I've put on my robe and slippers. I look at myself in the mirror on the wall. Then I take a deep breath and hold it.

I watch the second hand on my bedside clock. After

thirty seconds I'm dying, but I hold on. Forty seconds and I'm going to burst. Fifty-three seconds! But that's it. The best I can do. I stagger back to bed.

How will I ever hold my breath for two whole minutes?

That's what you have to do on Armistice Day if you go to the service up at the War Memorial. I saw it once on television. At exactly eleven o'clock on the eleventh day of the eleventh month, everybody at the service has to hold their breath for two minutes of silence. Even if you're only eleven and your father suddenly decides you've got to be a man and you're not ready.

I sit on my bed and try to think of an illness I can pretend to have that I haven't pretended to have recently.

That's when the caterwauling starts.

I tiptoe down the stairs to the second floor. It's Dad. I tiptoe along the hall to the staircase that leads to the main floor. My three older sisters are eavesdropping there.

Annie Oakley turns and glares at me.

"Shhhhhh," she whispers.

"Don't shhhhhh so loudly," says Letitia.

"God, you children are hopeless!" says Cassiopeia, the eldest.

We might end up having World War III right here on the stairs, but my father's voice interrupts the whispering war.

"Two-thirty?" he shouts. "Two-bloody-thirty-o'-bloody-o'clock?"

"Darling," says Mum.

"Don't darling me," says Dad. Then Rupert the Sausage starts to cry. He cries all the time. I lean way over the railing and I can just see him at the end of the hall in the kitchen in his high chair. My little sister, Flora Bella, is standing beside him. It looks as if she just poured orange juice on his head.

Dad marches out of the kitchen and down the hall. We skitter back up the stairs to the landing. He opens the door to his study, which is right at the bottom of the stairs. He doesn't notice us. He's dressed for the big event in a blazer with his war medals on it and a weird little soldier's cap I've never seen before. He shouts back down the hallway.

"Two-thirty! Is nothing sacred?" Then the study door slams shut behind him.

It's the day of the truce, but you wouldn't know it at our house.

Dad won't come out of his study and Mum is fuming, and it's all because they changed the ceremony up at the War Memorial to the afternoon.

"It's so people can go to church," Mum explains to us as she swabs up orange juice and tries to stop the Sausage from crying. "It's not usually on a Sunday."

"Yes it is," says Annie Oakley. "Every seven years it's on a Sunday."

"Well, I just wish Daddy would make us breakfast," says Cassiopeia. "Sunday is his day to make breakfast—the *only* day he makes breakfast."

"Oh, for God's sake, young lady," says Mum. "You're twenty years old. Make it yourself."

"No, it's the principle of the thing," says Cassiopeia. "He won't let *us* off the hook when we're in a bad mood."

"We could make breakfast together," says Letitia hopefully. "It would be fun."

Meanwhile, Annie has gone and got her bow and arrows from the front closet. She stomps past us toward the kitchen door. "Good idea," she says. "I'll go kill us a cat."

"Don't you dare!" says Mum.

"Okay, a squirrel," says Annie, and slams the back door behind her. It's ten o'clock on a Sunday morning and there have already been two slammed doors. This is getting interesting.

"I thought we had some rules around here about not going out on Sundays," says Cassiopeia to Mum, who only glares at her as she rinses out an orange-juice-soaked tea towel in the sink.

"I know how to make cinnamon toast," says Letitia. "We learned in home ec."

"I want sausages," says Flora Bella. Then she turns her gleaming eyes on our baby brother sitting in his high chair. She grabs him by his fat knees. "I want *these* sausages!"

The Sausage had just stopped crying, but now he's off again.

"That's it!" cries Mum, throwing up her hands. "I quit."

And as we all watch in shocked silence, she heads up the hall to the stairs, throwing her apron on the floor as she goes.

"Make your own breakfast, shoot as many squirrels as you like. I'm through with the lot of you!" She is passing the study and she raises her voice so that the ogre with the medals and the funny hat on the other side of the door hears her loud and clear.

It's so exciting! Like Jackie Gleason and Audrey Meadows on *The Honeymooners*. My mind is working overtime. I run up the stairs after my mother. "Can I go out?" I ask.

"*May* I go out!" says Mum.

"*May* I go out?"

"You may go to Hartford and Hereford and Hampshire as far as I'm concerned." She slams the master bedroom door shut.

A three-slammed-door morning! The new world record.

Before anyone can say another word I scoot up to my room to put on my outside clothes. My blazer, gray flannel pants, white shirt, and red tie are all freshly ironed and carefully draped over the chair in the corner of my room, waiting for the Armistice Day service. I salute my good clothes as I pick up my Saturday things lying in a heap on the floor. My jeans are still a bit damp from yesterday, but who cares. Then I dash down the stairs before my parents come to their senses.

For some strange reason, we are never allowed to play outside on Sundays. I don't know why. We're not religious. We don't go to church, anyway. We're supposed to stay in, or maybe go for a car ride or something dull like that. So this is too good to be true.

And it isn't.

Cassiopeia is waiting for me, guarding the front door.

"Where do you think you're going?" she demands. Her arms are crossed on her chest. She looks just like a grownup. Actually, I can't ever remember her being a kid.

"Mum said I could go out," I say, trying to push past her.

"You know the rules," she says. "No playing on Sunday."

I wish she'd get married and have kids of her own to boss around. And that's when I remember Mr. Odsburg. He works with her at the jewelry store and now they're dating. I step up close to her, so close her perfume almost knocks me out.

"You try to stop me and I'll tell Mum about last Friday."

"What's that supposed to mean?"

"On the porch. After midnight." I pull my arm up to my mouth and start smooching it until she gasps.

"What were you doing up?"

"It doesn't matter."

"You were spying—"

"I'll tell her *everything*."

"You are despicable," she says, but I can hear the quavering in her voice. She's going to cave in. And sure enough, she slouches against the doorjamb. It's as if she is Superman and I just waved a big fat chunk of kryptonite in her face. I fly down the porch steps, scooping up my bike.

I'm free.

THE LITTLE BLACK BOOK

I t's like visiting a new country. The country of Sunday. It looks mostly the same on my street but there are more hats. Churchgoers in hats, holding them down against the November wind.

It's cold. I've got a sweater on but I wish I'd grabbed my jacket. I put my Raleigh into third and pump hard to keep warm. I turn south off Clemow onto Bank Street. It's almost empty of traffic. So this is what Sunday is like.

I stop at the phone booth at First and check for nickels. None. I stop again at Third. I do this all the time and I've found one dollar and thirty-five cents since we moved here in July.

Taking money someone forgot doesn't seem like stealing most days, but it does on Sunday. And here's the thing: where am I going to spend it? Nothing is open. Nothing except church.

Anyway, all these thoughts are going through my head

as I reach the phone booth at Fifth. I dump my bike and pull back the accordion door. I pull down the change thingie.

Empty.

Then I see the book.

It's a little black book sitting on the shelf beside the phone. An address book with gold tabs for every letter of the alphabet, even X.

I thumb through to X. Nobody named X. No X men. But that makes me think of something else and I flip back to M: Manderley, Mathers, Morrison, Mumford. There are two pages of M names but no Mxyzptlk. He's Superman's arch-enemy. So, obviously, this isn't Clark Kent's address book. He didn't leave it here when he stepped inside to transform into a superhero. What happens to his everyday clothes when he does that? What a great discovery that would be: stepping into a phone booth and finding the suit of a mild-mannered reporter for the *Daily Planet* lying on the floor.

I flip through the address book and then close it quickly, feeling guilty, as if I were reading one of my sister's diaries.

What am I supposed to do? It's a dilemma. Leave it or take it? I lean my forehead against the phone and think hard. I look at the book again. Open it to N, just to see if by any chance the person who lost this book knows us. Nope. No Norton-Nortons. But that gives me an idea. The address book is bursting with clues—in fact, every page is a clue!

All of the people in this book know the person who owns it.

I bet if I sat down and really looked it over carefully, like Sherlock Holmes, I could figure out who that mysterious person is. That would be unbelievably great! I can see myself knocking on a door and handing the book to Miss X.

"How did you ever do it!" the woman cries in amazement.

"Deductuation, ma'am," I say. "No, no reward necessary. A dollar? Well, if you insist. Thank you."

"No," says the woman, her face aglow with happiness. "Thank *you*, Rex Zero."

Rex Zero is the name Buster and James gave me the first day we met, last summer. Buster thought the hyphen in my name was a minus sign, which meant I was Rex Norton minus Norton, or Rex Zero! It's a good name for a hero—or for a detective who deductuates dilemmas.

Bang, bang, bang.

I almost leap out of my skin. I turn around and gasp. There's this freckly red face with a red flattop and a yellow peewee football clenched between its teeth pressed up against the glass door.

It's Buster! I pocket the address book and pull back the door.

"I was just thinking about you," I say.

He takes the football out of his mouth. "What are you doing out on a Sunday? Did you run away from home? Was your family all mysteriously gassed in the night and now you're an orphan?"

I smile mysteriously. I'm Rex Zero—I'll never tell!

It turns out there's supposed to be a game down near the canal on this abandoned field across from Lansdowne Park. We ride over. The field is next to an old-folks home with a huge vegetable garden. No one's there.

"Oh, right," says Buster. "The game's not until one."

So we head south over the Rideau Canal, past the library, past the Mercury dealership, where there's a brand-new gold Mercury Monterey convertible in the window. *Varooom!*

Finally we come to the Rideau River. It's way bigger than the canal. I've never gone this far before. We stop on the bridge and throw stuff in the water—twigs, rocks, a dead running shoe. Then we cross over.

"Are we still in Ottawa?" I ask.

Buster shakes his head. "Nope," he says. "This is West Dakota."

I suppose he means South Dakota. Buster isn't good on geography.

We take off up Riverside Drive until Buster's not sure where we are anymore, which is a good time to head back. It's uphill all the way but that's no problem when you've got a three-speed.

When at last we get back to the field, there are some guys chucking a peewee football around.

I see James, Sami, Walli—Sami's younger brother—and some other kids from school. Eight guys in all. Little Donnie Dangerfield is there. He's in my class—the class clown. Right now he's standing on his head. He wants James to throw the ball at him so he can catch it with his feet.

Then I see the new guy. He arrived at school only a few weeks ago from Hungary. He has this great name, Zoltan Kádár. Some guys have all the luck.

There were troubles in Hungary—a war of some kind. Something to do with the Reds. Figures. Everything bad these days has to do with the Reds. But Zoltan's family escaped, which makes him pretty interesting.

"I don't believe it!" says James when he sees me. "You're out on a Sunday. What happened?"

He throws me the ball and I catch it, no problem. I'm pretty good at football. I don't look like I'd be good at anything athletic because I'm so skinny. But I'm fast and I've got soft hands.

They put Zoltan guarding me. He's older than us, I think, and pretty tall, but he's just learning about our kind of football.

James is the quarterback of the other team. He takes the snap and steps back in the pocket. We all have to count to six steamboats before Walli can attack. You have to count one steamboat, two steamboats—like that, to give the quarterback some time. Anyway, James's teammates run around in circles, jumping up and down and yelling for him to throw the ball.

"Jimbo, Jimbo!"

"Here, here, here!"

Zoltan doesn't yell. In fact he hasn't left the line of scrimmage. At first I figure he doesn't understand. Then I realize that he's looking for something. His key? Or maybe a precious piece of jewelry his dying father gave him back in Hungary before the Reds blew up their house? He's patting his pockets and his eyes are sweeping the brown and stunted grass. I start looking, too, and the next thing I know—he's bolted!

James tosses a little squib of a pass and Zoltan goes for big yards. It was a play! They tricked me. Zoltan smiles like a wolf as he heads back to the huddle.

It won't happen again, Boltin' Zoltan!

I get the chance to pay him back about four possessions later. I stumble making a catch. It's not a big deal but Zoltan grabs on to my arm to stop me from falling. "You good?" he asks.

"Yeah, I'm okay."

And then I take a step and wince with pain. He reaches out again to take my arm. I wave him off.

"It's just my ankle," I tell him. I lift my right leg and slowly turn my foot a couple of times both ways. I wince a little more and then hobble back to the huddle.

The next play I take off on a down-and-out, but I pull up lame and the ball sails over my head.

"Sorry, guys," I say as I limp back to the huddle and give Ernie, our quarterback, a sly wink.

He doesn't throw the ball to me again for two possessions. Every time I go out on a pattern I hop around a bit and never get free.

Then we're about thirty yards from the end zone.

"You ready, Zero?" mutters Ernie.

I nod.

Everybody goes wide right and wide left. I run a post pattern, slowly at first and then—

Fwooop! I take off.

I'm a stock car smoking up the pavement. I hear Zoltan behind me yelling something in Hungarian. It sounds like a swearword! He's after me, but I've got the jump on him and Ernie's got me in his sights. It's a bomb, all right, but a little short. I turn to meet it and then realize the wind is giving it some lift. I have to run backward—fast! And all the time Zoltan is getting nearer and nearer, yelling things in Hungarian.

I leap, arms stretched, and come down with the ball, but I'm going backward so fast I fall.

Right into the end zone.

Touchdown!

Zoltan comes up, breathing hard, and stands over me with his fists on his hips. I just lie there catching my breath, not sure what he's going to do.

Then he grins. "Good trick."

He offers me his hand. I reach out and he snatches it away so that I tumble over again on my backside.

"Good trick," I say.

And he laughs as he heads back to the gang.

I feel good. Ottawa may have lost the quarterfinals yesterday, but the pride of the city has just been saved by skinny, but oh so crafty, Rex Zero.

When I'm on my feet, I see that the little black book I found in the phone booth is lying on the ground. I pick it up and stick it back in my pants pocket.

I'm facing the garden of the old-folks home. An old man is in the garden, wearing gray pants, a blazer, and a beret. Apart from the beret, it's exactly what Mum had set out for me to wear.

The old guy is standing, facing north, and he's saluting. Maybe he's crazy.

Then it hits me.

Hits me like a truckload of frozen pumpkins.

I don't have a watch. But the old man knows what time it is. He's holding his breath and facing in the direction of the National War Monument up near Parliament Hill, as if he could see it two miles away.

It's the middle of the afternoon, but it's the eleventh hour for me!

THE FIRST CLUE

enter the house by the basement stairs. I'll have to face the music sometime but I want to lie low for a while and try to get a sense of the lay of the land. If I hear screaming and yelling upstairs, maybe I'll just stay in the basement until I'm old enough to get a place of my own.

I head straight for the House of Punch. That's this bomb shelter my sister Annie Oakley built out of *Punch* magazines that she piled up around a huge table in the middle of the room. Now there's this little room inside the big room. She lets me hang out there, sometimes, and between us we've made it pretty comfortable with an old carpet and pillows.

She's there.

"Boy, are you in trouble," she says. Even in the dull light under the table, I can see her eyes gleam with satisfaction.

"I didn't mean to miss it," I say. "I lost my watch."

"Oh, well then, I'm sure Dad won't be mad."

She's right. I'm going to have to come up with something better.

"So Dad went anyway?"

"Of course."

"Alone?"

"Yep. I asked if I could go but it had to be number one son." She sounds angry, but she's angry nearly all the time. "I told Daddy I want to be a soldier one day. He didn't even care. It was Rex or nobody."

I try to imagine Annie in uniform, fighting in hand-to-hand combat against some huge Nazi storm trooper. The Nazi is looking pretty worried.

"What do you think Dad will do?" I ask.

I must sound really scared because she takes pity on me.

"He's not so mad as he is sad," she says.

"Oh, great."

"Yeah," she says. "But it's more than that. He's always sad around Armistice Day. Didn't you ever notice? He goes into a genuine, A-one, blue funk. He'll be quiet as a mouse one minute and yelling the next."

I think about it. She's right. "I guess he's remembering friends who got killed," I say.

She shrugs her shoulders. I can tell there's more she wants to say but I bite my lip. You can't press Annie Oakley, not unless you want an arrow up the nose.

"Last year," she says, "he was napping on the couch, right around Armistice Day. He looked like he was having some kind of a nightmare. I watched. I went up really close. I was just going to wake him up when he said something—not to me—but I almost thought it was, because his voice was so clear. It sounded like he was yelling a warning. Like he was saying don't do that or don't go out there, or something."

"But you couldn't understand what he was saying?"

She shakes her head. "No," she says. Then she looks right into my eyes and wraps her hand around my wrist. Her fingers are icy cold. "I couldn't understand him," she whispers, "because he was talking in *German*."

◎ ◎ ◎

Mum is at the sink when I go upstairs. She doesn't turn around but she knows it's me.

"Wait in your room until your father comes home."

I don't answer. I turn toward the hall and leave. I want to say something like "See how good I'm being, not arguing or making up excuses or anything?" But I can't say that. When you're trying to act mature you're not allowed to point it out.

In my room I think about Dad talking German. Where did he learn German? Maybe Annie got it wrong. He could have been talking Welsh. He knows Welsh because he was born in Wales. But Annie knows what Welsh sounds like. And she knows what German sounds like, too.

I sit on my bed with my pillows piled up behind me. As soon as I sit down I'm aware of the secret in my pocket because it pokes me.

I dig it out and start reading through it, looking for clues. Whenever I see a phone number that starts with CE, I look especially hard. The CE stands for Central. Our number is CE 5-6334.

In the E section, I find Harold Ermanovics on Percy Avenue. There's a Sandy Ermanovics at school. I don't know where he lives but it might be on Percy. I look at the number. It's worth a try. I know I'm supposed to stay in my room but I'm dying of curiosity. Besides, sitting in your room is like waiting for the jailer to come with the last supper, before they fry you in the chair.

What if I phone Sandy and his dad just happens to know somebody who was complaining about missing his address book? The mystery would be solved, just like that. And then I could tell my father that I was really sorry about missing Armistice Day, but I had made somebody very happy. Maybe then I'd only get ten years of hard labor instead of the electric chair.

We have two phones now, which gives me some options. One phone is in the front hall and the other is in

Dad's study. I'll need privacy for this mission. If Mum catches me, I'll get the electric chair twice!

I sneak down the stairs.

Cassiopeia and Letitia are in their shared bedroom—probably making up the names of the men they are going to marry. Annie must still be in the House of Punch. Mum is in the kitchen. She's turned up the stereo and is listening to her latest LP from the Columbia Record Club. Dinah Shore, *A Swingin' Tour of the Sunny South.* The music is loud enough to cover the noise of me sneaking down the stairs.

I peek into the living room. Flora Bella is trying to hula hoop to Dinah singing "Mississippi Mud." She is concentrating hard, which is good. The last thing I need is Flora Bella around when I'm trying to make a secret phone call. The Sausage is on the living room floor playing with a piece of raw spaghetti. He loves raw spaghetti. He's talking to it. Telling the spaghetti his problems.

I slip into my father's study and gently close the door behind me. I go straight to his desk, and before I lose my courage altogether, I pull out the little black book and dial Sandy's number.

"Hello?"

It's a girl—a sister, I guess.

"Is Sandy there?"

She goes to get him.

"Hello?"

"Sandy?"

"Uh-huh."

"Hi, it's Rex Norton-Norton." No response. "From school?" No response. "Remember I traded you Kenny Ploen for Sam Etcheverry?" Still nothing. "They're quarterbacks, one with the Blue Bombers—"

"I know who *they* are. I'm just not sure who *you* are."

"I'm a friend of Sami Karami's."

"Oh, yeah," he says. Everyone knows Sami. "What do you want?"

"I found an address book and your father's name was in it." Another pause. "I'm trying to find the owner and the only clue I've got so far is that your father's name is in the book."

"So?"

It's beginning to dawn on me how hard this is going to be.

"Well, I just thought that whoever the person is who lost the address book might have said something and your dad would remember and then he could tell me who it was and I could give it back."

There is another pause. A long one. Then Sandy says, "What?"

Sheesh!

"Well, I just thought maybe you could ask your father if he knows anyone who lost his address book." I'm struck by a sudden idea—the owner could be a woman. And so I say, "And maybe ask your mother, too."

"Okay," he says. But he doesn't sound very enthusiastic. "See you."

"Yeah," I say. "Tomorrow."

I hang up the phone and lean back in my father's chair. It's one of those chairs that swivel and tip. I swivel it a bit and tip it back. I put my feet up on Dad's desk. My hands are behind my head, just like Sam Spade in *The Maltese Falcon*. I imagine this doll in high heels standing at the door wringing her hands and crying about losing her husband. "I'll pay anything for you to track him down, Mr. Spade. Anything!"

And then, to my surprise, the door really does open and it isn't a doll in high heels. It's Major Dad. I sit up straight, as he closes the door behind him.

"Just the man I was looking for," he says.

THE CAMEMBERT CHEESE WAR

I scuttle away from Dad's desk and sit in the big green wingback chair in the corner. He doesn't say anything. He watches me scuttle and then turns his attention to the photographs on the wall over the bookcase. At first his hands are behind his back, at ease. And then, after about sixteen thousand hours, he fishes in his blazer pocket for his pipe and tobacco.

I sit perfectly still, my feet on the floor, my back straight. I think about what I'll order for my last supper. Probably steak-and-kidney pie. I hate steak-and-kidney pie. One mouthful and I'll be saying, "Somebody execute me—please."

But it begins to look as if Dad has Chinese water torture in mind. Slowly he fills his pipe. *Drip, drip.* Looks at the picture of his army platoon. *Drip, drip.* The handsome picture of him in uniform that was used as a poster during the war. *Drip, drip.*

I can't take it anymore.

"Did anybody faint?" I ask.

He glances my way almost as if he had forgotten I was there.

"Not that I noticed. It's usually only hot weather that brings a soldier to his knees."

"I just thought with holding your breath and everything."

"Holding your breath?"

"For two minutes. The best I can manage is fifty-three seconds."

"Good grief, Rex. It's two minutes of *silence*. Just because you don't talk for two minutes doesn't mean you can't breathe. Besides if you'd managed to get there, you'd have seen that everyone was fitted out with a scuba tank before the ceremony. Everyone except for Dief the Chief, of course."

"Really?"

"Yes. It's tradition. The prime minister never gets the scuba tank. They figure politicians are so full of hot air they'll be fine."

There he is, making jokes again when he's in a bad mood. I can tell he's in a bad mood because his eyes seem to be peering out at me from two little caves under an outcropping of granite. And those eyebrows of his—they're just writhing!

"I'm really sorry, Dad."

He puffs on his pipe. "I'm sorry, too, son." He sounds so sad.

"I didn't forget on purpose. Honest. I just lost track of time."

He nods, almost absentmindedly. He's keeping his temper under wraps. I'm not sure if that's a good thing or a bad thing.

"Slippery thing, time," he says. "It should come with a good firm handle, don't you think?"

"Yes, sir."

"In the war I lost track of time a lot. We all did. We'd sometimes have to set up search parties to go looking for it. We'd get the radio operator radioing back to headquarters in case we'd left it there. We'd check out on the battlefield, in case some enemy soldier had done a runner with our platoon's supply. The enemy was clever that way. Used up a lot of our time and never once asked permission. Eventually, someone would find it stuffed under his cot—'Oh, here it is, sir. Sorry about that. It got stuck behind this packet from home. Biscuit, anyone?' So we'd all have a biscuit from home and get back to work because we knew what time it was again and we knew there wasn't any to lose."

There's a lesson in Dad's story, but I'm not sure what it is. All I can think about is the packet from home with the biscuits in it.

"What were you up to?" he says. "Driving the hombres out of Dry Gulch, again?"

"No, sir. I'm a little old for cowboys and Indians."

"Ah, well then, was it a girl?"

"Dad, cut it out!"

That's when he sits down at his desk. "So tell me," he says. And there is no humor left in his voice.

I tell him everything—or almost. I don't tell him about the address book. But I tell him about tricking Zoltan by pretending I was lame and then scoring the winning touchdown.

"Deked him out of his jockstrap, did you?"

"Yes, sir."

"Good. Good," he says. But his eyes drift away, behind a plume of smoke, toward the pictures on the wall.

"We played a fair amount of football in the war," he says. "Real football—soccer—not this gridiron nonsense. Of course, that was only on the days when Jerry's mother showed up and dragged him home by the ear to clean his room."

"Jerry?"

"The Germans."

He gets up again and wanders back to the wall. He points at a face among the thirty or forty soldiers in his platoon.

"This fellow here, Quincy, he could deke anybody. He played for England once."

"Is that true?"

"Yes," says Dad, glaring at me. "I'll alert you when I'm lying."

"Sorry," I say quickly. The thing is, Dad is always making up stories. But there is an edge in his voice and I don't want him to trip over it and fall into a full-fledged temper.

"Good old Quincy," he says after a minute, tapping the little figure in the regimental portrait. "Lost a leg in the final push. Then he could only deke out half of us."

I don't laugh. Instead, I look at the picture. I can't see Quincy from where I'm sitting; he's too small. But I can see Dad because he's dead center. Major Dad, a sapper, which means a Royal Engineer in the British Army.

I glance up. Dad's smiling again. Not at me. At his boys. The family he had before us.

"The chap who shot Quincy got his just deserts—died an odd sort of death. Very messy. I wonder if I ever told you about it."

I shake my head.

"Ah, well," he says, and returns to his desk. He takes off his blazer and rolls up his sleeves. I wonder if he's going to *show* me how the soldier died! But he sits down and puts his feet up just the way I was doing when he walked in. He tips back his chair and knits his fingers together behind his head.

"It was a sniper incident, a few days after the invasion. We'd just built a bridge across the Touques River, near Vimoutiers. We hardly had it finished before the troops were rolling across it, pressing on toward Berlin. That's what sappers do, Rex, keep the troops moving."

"Yes, sir," I say. But I don't feel as if he is really talking to me anymore. He seems a long way away.

"Suddenly, there was rifle fire. Two went down before we knew what hit us. Quincy was one of them."

I sit forward in my seat as if I've just heard the gunshots.

"The shots came from an abandoned farm. We took cover as best we could, fired back, and gradually sorted out where Jerry was holed up. It seemed there was only one shooter. But he had the high ground and open fields all around him. After a while, we figured he wasn't in the old house or the barn but a small outbuilding. Under cover fire I made my way on my belly along the culvert beside the road and then through the tall grass along the fence line due south of him. When I was sure I was out of eyeshot, I circled around to come at him from the rear. My men kept him busy while I crept closer and closer. It was a smallish shed with a Dutch door. The top section of the door was open. The sun was setting and hitting the front of the shed full on. I could see dust puffing out the top part of the door. But I couldn't see my quarry."

His voice grows quiet, as if he doesn't dare speak any louder or Jerry will hear. Hugging myself, I settle back into the protective arms of the wingback chair.

"I slithered along the shed wall until I was right below the door opening. Then—quick as a fox—I lobbed a grenade inside and ran like a madman.

"*Boom!* I covered my head as bits of the shed rained down on me. And do you know what else?"

I shake my head, though I have a bad feeling.

Dad's eyes open wide and he grins like a mad scientist. "Camembert cheese!" he says.

"What?"

"Camembert cheese, lad."

Another joke. Why does he do this? I guess I must look a bit annoyed.

"God's truth," he says, crossing his heart. "The shed was full of it."

I search his face. He looks sincere. "Is that the runny kind of cheese?"

"The very same! It was everywhere, Rex. It was raining Camembert."

"Yuck."

"Oh, that wasn't all. It was raining Camembert *and* German soldier. Can you imagine it, Rex?"

I can. It's sort of funny but not funny. Just like Quincy deking people out on one leg is funny but not funny.

His eyes are miles away and suddenly I miss him. I should have been with him at the War Memorial. I wish I could get that time back. I wish he would *come* back. Back from that field in France, even if he is all covered with smelly cheese and German soldier and Mum makes him take off his clothes on the porch, like she does when I get home from playing.

I wish he'd come home and talk to me. *Really* talk to me.

He leans back in his chair. His pipe has gone out.

"It takes seven pints of raw milk to make one round of Camembert," he says. "And it's not an easy cheese to make, I gather. It requires real craftsmanship and time. A good long time to ripen it." He shakes his head sadly.

"Such a waste, don't you think, Rex?"

He looks me square in the face, and he smiles, but there is a tear in his eye.

I sit perfectly still and hold my breath. Right now I'm sure I can go two minutes. It's the least I can do.

MISS GARR

When Miss Garr replaced Miss Cinnamon, Annie said, "I hear she kills about two students a year."

"Oh, surely not," said Mum. "One, perhaps. That's only to be expected."

"She's pretty scary," I said. "She keeps threatening to use the strap if we don't watch our step."

"Well, stay on her good side," said Mum. "Does she have a good side?"

I shrugged. "She seems to like me okay. She said I was the kind of boy who wasn't in any hurry to grow up."

"And that's supposed to be a good thing?" said Annie.

◎ ◎ ◎

On the Monday after Armistice Day we have a class council meeting. Somehow I get elected secretary. That might be because my handwriting is good. Or it might be because nobody else wanted the job. Sami is treasurer because he is the best in the class at math. And Polly Goldstein is the class president.

It's hard being secretary because you're writing all the time. But today I'm glad. My head is buzzing with too many ideas. Dad didn't punish me for missing Armistice Day, but he didn't really forgive me, either. I left him in his study and he didn't come out again until dinner. And he was quiet at dinner, which isn't like him.

"Rex? Are you getting this down?" Miss Garr suddenly says.

Council has already been called to order. This is how it goes: Polly brings up items on the agenda that Miss Garr has written out for her. Then Miss Garr tells us how we're going to vote on each item. Sometimes there's a question from the floor—that's what you call the class when it's having a council meeting, as if we're all supposed to be lying down. When that happens, the person always asks Miss Garr and she always says, "You should address that question to your elected representative." So the person on the floor asks Polly, but before she can answer, Miss Garr usually answers for her.

There are two things to discuss on the agenda today. We are going to have a raffle to raise money for a Christmas party. We suggest things that would be a good prize: a new bike (Kathy), a box of chocolates (Susan-Anne-Margaret), tickets to an Ottawa-Hull Junior Canadiens hockey game

(Marv), and a trip for two to Las Vegas (Donnie). We all laugh, but Miss Garr looks down as if she is searching for a rock to throw at Donnie.

When she starts looking for rocks, we stop laughing pretty quickly because we know she is in Stage One of getting angry. When she looks up again we decide that the raffle prize will be a basket of yummy Christmas biscuits and fruit that Miss Garr can get cheaply from her brother's store.

"We will need to have the raffle tickets printed up by a fortnight from now. Does anyone know what a fortnight is?"

"Two weeks," I say.

She smiles. "Next time put up your hand first, dear," she says.

So I stick up my hand.

"Yes, Rex?"

"Yes, ma'am," I reply.

People start to titter. Donnie Dangerfield laughs out loud.

"Enough!" says Miss Garr. Then she looks at me with this hurt expression as if I've really disappointed her. I quickly write down the date when we have to have the raffle tickets printed in my secretarial notes. I count out fourteen on my fingers and write down November the twenty-sixth. I try to concentrate, but I start thinking about what Annie said in the House of Punch, about Dad always getting sad around this time of year. How long does the sadness last? Is there something we should do? Dress up in costumes? Put on a puppet show?

"Rex! What has gotten into you?"

"Sor . . ." I put up my hand and wait for her to nod. "Sorry, Miss Garr." Then I lower my hand. Kathy, who sits across the aisle from me, tells me what I missed.

Miss Garr is frowning. She takes what she calls one of her "deep restorative breaths."

"Now, Polly, ask the class what would be a good day for the Christmas Party—the day we make the draw for the raffle?"

Polly frowns and stands up. "What would be a good day for the Christmas Party—the day we make the draw for the raffle?" she asks.

"Polly? Did I detect a note of sarcasm in your voice?"

"No, ma'am," says Polly. She turns to the class. "Any ideas?" Nobody has any ideas because we are pretty sure Miss Garr has already decided. Then Polly turns to the front. "I think the last day of classes would be good."

Miss Garr smiles but her left eyebrow arches. "Polly, Polly, Polly. Have we forgotten about the democratic principle?"

"Nobody had any suggestions, Miss Garr. And just because I'm president doesn't mean I don't get a vote."

"The last day would be keen!" says Donnie. "Then we can have games and cake and fool around, and not worry about the room getting all messy."

There is a buzz of approval that is squelched by Miss Garr. "Unfortunately, I have other plans for the last day of class."

"A human sacrifice," someone whispers.

"What was that?"

No one answers.

Miss Garr turns her gaze toward the last row, over by the window. Donnie sits in the second to last seat. "I presume that was you, Donnie," she says. "It seems you are determined to make a mockery of these proceedings."

"It wasn't me," says Donnie. "But what *do* you have planned for the last day of classes?"

I look down at my notes. I'm not sure if I should write any of this down. Things are getting out of hand.

"Polly!" says Miss Garr. "Please call this meeting to order."

Polly pounds the toy gavel on her desk. "Order," she says.

"Thank you," says Miss Garr. "Now the party date I would like to suggest, if I may, would be exactly a week after we distribute the raffle tickets." She doesn't even bother to ask for a vote this time. She turns to me and says, "Please enter that in the minutes, Rex."

I'm just about to start when Polly interrupts. "Excuse me, Miss Garr. But that would be a bad date for me, personally. I won't be able to be here."

Miss Garr looks annoyed at first and then her expression changes so that she looks like a person trying to be considerate. "Ah, yes. I see. Is that the date your people start their own special midwinter celebration?"

Your people?

Everyone stares at Polly, who looks embarrassed. "If you mean Hanukkah, no it isn't that. I have to get my new braces that day."

Some people laugh. And Miss Garr looks like she's in Stage Two of getting angry. She is searching the floor for big rocks now. Silence descends like mustard gas on the class.

"I'm sorry, Polly. But the date for the party is firm due to all kinds of reasons beyond our control and which there is not time to discuss here." She looks up and manages a smile, though it looks like she found it secondhand at the Salvation Army store.

"So, Rex?" Miss Garr is looking my way. "Do you have that entered in the minutes?"

I'm not sure what she's talking about.

"The date of the party," Kathy whispers.

"Oh. Yes, ma'am." Did she say a week? I count it out quickly on my fingers and write it down.

"Could you read it back to us, please, Mr. Secretary?"

I stand up and read from my notes. "The class party will be on November the thirty-third."

Everyone goes crazy. For a moment I'm surprised and then I realize what I've done and slap myself in the forehead. That makes everyone go even crazier.

But no one goes crazy like Donnie Dangerfield. He's actually rolling on the floor. I love that. Meanwhile, Sami is circling his ear with his finger and his eyes are all googly, and Polly smiles back at me in a really nice way, as if I've done something wonderful. Even Zoltan seems to get the joke and is nodding his head.

"Class! Class!! *Class!!!*"

When Miss Garr says "Class" three times, we have reached Stage Three and we are *all* in imminent danger. We pipe down quickly.

She walks over to the window aisle and stares hard at Donnie. He gets up off the floor and takes his seat. He's still smiling, which is probably not such a good idea.

"Do you think it is polite, Donald, to put on such a show of disrespect because of the stupidity of a fellow classmate?"

Donnie looks surprised. "No, ma'am. I wasn't laughing because what Rex said was stupid. I was laughing because it was funny."

"Have you no concern for his feelings?"

Yikes!

Donnie glances over at me across the room. He makes a face as if it had never occurred to him that my feelings would be hurt. I hold up my hands to apologize for getting him in trouble. The class is silent. Finally, Donnie sighs. But says nothing.

"You will answer me, young man."

Donnie looks down at his desk and traces a pattern on the top of it with his finger. Then he looks up and his eyes are bright. "How about we put it to a vote?" he says. He immediately turns to Polly. "Can we vote on whether what Rex said was funny or stupid?"

Before Miss Garr can catch a restorative breath, Polly jumps to her feet. "I think it would be the democratic thing to do," she says.

"Now wait one minute," says Miss Garr. But everybody is turning toward Polly.

"Those who think that what Rex said was stupid, raise their hands," says Polly. Nobody raises a hand.

"Children! This has gone too far."

"Those who think that what Rex said was funny, raise their hands." Everybody raises their hands, including me. I glance at Miss Garr. She is leaning on the windowsill, her shoulders hunched like a vulture, staring out at the playground. I guess there just aren't big enough rocks in the classroom and she's looking for boulders!

"So it's carried," says Polly. Her face is flushed. She turns to me. "Enter it in the minutes, please, Rex."

"Don't you dare!" says Miss Garr.

Her face is like something from *Shock Theatre*. Her eyes are huge and her skin has gone all splotchy with angry red blotches.

There is dead silence. She tries to speak and can't. She

takes a deep breath and turns her attention to Donnie. We all turn our attention to Donnie. But I can't help wondering: why is she looking at him and not Polly?

"I don't know what your parents let you get away with at home, Donald Dangerfield, but you will not run roughshod over my classroom. You will apologize to Mr. Norton-Norton immediately for being so rude and callous as to laugh at him. Do you understand?"

Donnie doesn't look up.

"I said, do you understand? You know perfectly well what is going to happen if you do not do as I tell you."

Someone gasps. Probably Susan-Anne-Margaret, who is the most sensitive girl in the class.

Donnie is still tracing a pattern on his desk with his finger. Then just before Miss Garr can say another word, he looks up. You can see in his face that he has come to some huge decision.

"Miss Garr. No one in this class thought what Rex said was stupid except you." Now everyone gasps. "Don't you think *you're* the one who should apologize?"

Miss Garr has to lean on the windowsill for support. She is speechless. I write it in the minutes: *Miss Garr speechless.* This has never happened. I decide I am going to work on these minutes when I get home. They are going to be the best minutes ever. Suddenly, being the class secretary doesn't seem like a dull job at all.

When I look up again she is crossing the front of the

classroom toward her desk. She opens the bottom drawer and draws from it a thick green strap.

"No!" says Kathy, pretty loudly, but Miss Garr is beyond hearing. She straightens up and closes the bottom drawer with her foot.

It's the first time I've ever seen the strap, though she's mentioned it a bunch of times. It's all nobbly and looks like it is woven out of steel cable or something.

We sit back in our chairs as far as we can. It's as if she had taken a poisonous viper out of her desk.

"Miss Garr," says Polly.

"Sit down, young lady."

Polly sits, reluctantly. "Miss Garr," she says again, urgently. "It was my fault."

"Silence!" says Miss Garr, aiming a death ray at the class president.

Polly puts her hands together on her desktop and stares at the ink bottle hole. There are tears in her eyes. I will write those tears into the minutes later. But now I am frozen watching Miss Garr.

Everyone—everyone but Polly—is watching her. She has walked to the center of the room, the thick green belt clenched in her right hand, draped over the palm of the other like a tame snake.

"I could send you to the office, Donnie, and have Mr. Johnstone discipline you. But I think it just might make more of an impression if the punishment is meted out here before your classmates. Please come to the front of the room."

Donnie doesn't hesitate. He marches to the front of the room and stands before her, as straight as a soldier. She takes his shoulder and firmly moves him over to the side so that they are in profile to the class. "I'm sorry it had to come to this," she says.

I watch the first slap. She gives him three. I'm too busy writing to watch the last two. And too shaky to write anything you could actually read.

KATHY'S DILEMMA

November thirty-third? November thirty-third! Donnie's wrong. I *am* stupid." We're walking up Lyon Street after school. Except Kathy's not here. I don't know where she went.

"It wasn't your fault," says James.

"No way," says Buster. "Miss Cinnamon would never do something like that, would she?"

"No way," I say.

"Mr. Gallup wouldn't either," says Buster. "He'd say, 'What a good idea, Rex! Why should we remember all those months, eh? Why can't it just be January all year long? Let's have the class party on January the three-hundredth-and-thirty-seventh.' "

It's good to laugh. But it doesn't change the situation. If I hadn't been so wrapped up thinking about my own problems, Donnie wouldn't have gotten in trouble.

James stops all of a sudden. He looks like he's thinking hard, his eyes go all squinty. His hair is chocolate brown but he has this gray spot about the size of a quarter right in the middle above his forehead. Sometimes I think he is already partly a wise old man.

"What now?" says Buster.

James stares at him. "How did you do that?"

"Do what?"

"Figure out that the thirty-third of November—which is really the third of December—would be the three-hundred-and-thirty-fourth of January?"

"Three-hundred-and-thirty-*seventh*," says Buster. Then he scratches his head. "Would it?"

James shrugs. "I think so—something like that. But I'd need a piece of paper and a pencil to figure it out. And you just said it right out of your head."

"Maybe Buster is a genius," I say. That makes us all laugh, including Buster. Then we start walking again. It's gotten a lot cooler since yesterday. The sky is gray and as thick as a slab of concrete. It makes me think of that episode of *Superman* where he's trapped in a room and the ceiling starts coming down to crush him.

We head off up Lyon Street again, into the teeth of the wind. I bury my chin in my jacket.

"Hey, guys!"

We turn and there is Kathy. She runs to catch up.

"Where were you?" says Buster.

"I was talking to Polly. We were thinking up ways to kill Miss Garr."

"I'll help," says James.

"Then maybe Miss Cinnamon would come back," says Buster.

"I wish," says Kathy. "Why do people fall in love and ruin everything? It's stupid, stupid, stupid."

The rest of us look at one another with surprise.

"What's all this about?" says James.

Kathy pushes her hair out of her face. "Love," she says, as if love is something you might poke at with a long stick if you saw it lying in a gutter. Then she walks right past us.

We run to catch up to her. There is this huge scowl on her face. Her hair is flying around now like the wind is fighting over it. She gathers it in and tucks it under her scarf.

Something is up, something more than what happened in class.

"What's wrong?" I ask her.

She shrugs.

"Come on," says James. "Or we'll have to torture it out of you."

She makes a face. "I'm beyond torture," she says grumpily.

We guys share a glance and then Buster says, "I know. You bet a thousand dollars on the Rough Riders and you've got to come up with the money by six tonight or the Mafia is going to send you on a deep-six holiday in the Ottawa River."

Kathy's eyes warm up a little, but the flame isn't there.

Like when the kindling in the fireplace burns brightly but the logs just won't catch. "If I had a thousand dollars, I wouldn't waste it on some loser football team," she says.

And then I say, "Is something wrong with your mom?"

She sniffs and nods.

"How can there be anything wrong with your mom?" says Buster. "She's a nurse."

"Well, she's sick anyway," says Kathy. "Sick of me."

We are so surprised that no one can think of anything funny to say.

"Did you have a fight?" James asks.

"How could we have a fight when she's never around." Kathy crosses her arms on her chest. "She's seeing this man," she blurts out. "A doctor."

"So she *is* sick?" says Buster.

Kathy just glares at him.

"Do you mean she's *dating* someone?" says James.

Kathy snorts like a horse trying to blow away flies. "It makes me so mad!"

"Holy mackerel," says Buster. "Your mother is *dating*? She must be like thirty-five or something."

"That's exactly how old she is and it's disgusting, if you ask me."

"Is he horrible?"

She frowns again, shoves her hands into her pockets, and finds a crumpled-up Kleenex. She blows her nose. "He hasn't got horns and scales, if that's what you mean."

"Does he have a bolt through his neck?"

"No," says Kathy. "But he brings flowers."

"Oh, gross!"

"And chocolates. *Black Magic* chocolates."

"But I bet he never eats one," I say. "I bet he has very pale skin and long teeth and says, 'Not for me, my darlink. But a nice glass full of your *blood* would be most appreciated.' "

Kathy tries not to smile.

"Is it serious?" asks James. "Is he going to pop the question?"

Kathy glares at him. "Not if I can help it." Her voice is low and determined. When she gets like this she's pretty scary. "He's got a kid of his own, a daughter in kindergarten. At our school. I'm supposed to say hello to her and be nice."

"So his wife died?"

"No, she took off."

Took off? Like in a movie? Real people don't take off.

"It's true," says Kathy. "She just ran off with another man and left Dr. Arnold stranded with a baby girl."

"So did they get a divorce?" says Buster. "Because if they didn't get a divorce and he marries your mom, it will be bigamy, which is against the law, unless you're the Sheikh of Araby and you've got a harem."

Kathy frowns. "He got a divorce. Or he says he did."

I'm thinking back to something she said a few minutes ago. "You said your mom was sick of you. What do you mean?"

She shakes her head. "We had a fight. Dr. Arnold was coming over and I was supposed to help clean up the apartment. And she wanted me to do something about the shrine."

Kathy built this shrine to her father, who died in the Korean War. There are all these medals for bravery and Kathy has a little table with pictures of him and his medals and a flag. He died when she was a baby, but he wrote her all these letters while he was overseas.

"She wants you to take down the shrine to your dad?"

Kathy's shoulders fall. "Not take it down, exactly. Just . . . well, clean it up a bit. It's grown since you last saw it. I started putting up more pictures and old stuff of his. His pilot's helmet and, you know, some other things. His air force uniform." She pauses. "I guess the shrine got kind of large."

Kathy's apartment isn't very big. I'm trying to imagine how much of the room the shrine has taken over.

"I don't want Mom to forget about him," she says. "So I put everything I could find right out in the open. She says there isn't anywhere to sit. I just wanted Dr. Arnold to know."

There is a pause and then James says, "Is his name really Arnold?"

She nods. "Dr. Arnold Schwartz. His daughter's name is Missy. I'm supposed to be nice to Missy." She says Missy as if it was Kissy.

"Dr. Arnold," says Buster. "I bet he's not as brave as your father. I bet *he* didn't get shot down."

Nobody can think of anything else to say. I wonder if the other guys are thinking the same thing I'm thinking. I'm trying to imagine my mother going out on a date! It's too ridiculous for words.

It's just about then that I realize we've walked right past Clemow Avenue, which is where Buster and James and I all live. We've reached the entranceway to Adams Park. It's empty now. Desolate. There are puddles of water left over from the rain on Saturday and there are frozen clumps of dead leaves everywhere.

Kathy sighs and we all look at her.

"Do you want us to walk you home?" James asks.

She shakes her head. Then she looks at him and smiles. "Thanks anyway," she says. She turns to Buster and me. "Thanks, guys." She still looks sad but not *as* sad. "See you later." Then she turns north and heads off as if she's in a hurry. Maybe she's going to go home and clean up the shrine, like her mom wants her to. But I don't think so. There was a glint in her eye. Maybe she's going to turn the whole apartment into a shrine. Maybe she'll go to the air force and ask them to loan her an F-86 Sabre like the one her dad flew.

That ought to make Dr. Arnold feel welcome.

THE WOMAN IN WHITE

Buster is really rich and has lots of great toys and games, but the best thing about going to his house is that there's no one there. Sometimes a maid answers the door, but she always goes away and leaves you alone. Sometimes you can hear his mom somewhere laughing as if she's having a party all by herself, but she hardly ever makes an appearance, and when she does she never remembers any of our names. Buster's brother, Clem, is never at home. He's on the football team and the basketball team and the swim team and the ski team and the hopscotch team, for all I know. And as for Buster's dad, he's nearly always away on business trips. It's great!

We go to Buster's after we leave Kathy. We make Nestlé's Quik and put about three pounds of rainbow-colored miniature marshmallows in it. Then we put chocolate sprinkles and nuts and sugar and caramel sauce on top of that. When Buster gets out the mustard, ketchup, and corn relish, things get really crazy. We never actually end up drinking the Quik, but by then we are warmed up from laughing so much. And anyway, we find something better to snack on.

Buster's mother threw a bridge party and there are lots of little sandwiches in the fridge. They are about the size of stamps. Some are rolled up and some are diamond-shaped and some are round. There isn't a crust in sight! James and I try everything while Buster makes himself a macaroni loaf and Velveeta sandwich on Wonder Bread.

When Buster finally sits down, I tell him and James about the address book.

James flips through the book. "Well, here's what I think. This looks like a man's address book." I look at the book over his shoulder. "See how the writing leans forward?" he says. "A woman's writing always leans backward or it's straight up and down."

Boy oh boy, James is smart. If I do have a detective agency when I grow up I'll need him on board. "Besides," he adds, "women don't own black things. If this book belonged to a woman it would be pink or powder blue."

"You're right," I say. "Or yellow with a kitten on the front."

"That's not true," says Buster, wiping Velveeta off his lips with the edge of the tablecloth. "Women *do* have black things." He swallows his mouthful. "I found this magazine in my brother's room and it was full of pictures of women wearing black underwear."

"Are you sure?" I ask. None of my sisters wear black underwear.

Buster crosses his heart. Then he looks down at his sandwich with this glum look on his face. "I was sitting on his bed looking at the pictures when my mom came in. She sent me to bed with no supper."

"Just as well," says James. "Who could eat after seeing a lot of pictures of women wearing nothing but underwear?"

I nod. Sometimes my sisters walk around in their slips and they get all upset if I see them, and I have to tell Mum *I'm* the one who should be upset.

Buster's freckles start to flash like ambulance lights and he goes back to eating his sandwich.

"Could we phone some of the people in the book?" says James. Buster nods, his cheeks fat with sandwich. He points at the phone on the wall.

"There's about a thousand names," I say.

James turns back to A and goes down the list. "Okay, let's stick to the people who live in the Central exchange. Can I go first?"

"Sure."

So he drags his chair over to the phone and calls Alex Abelard. There's no answer. We agree that you get to make calls until you reach someone. He calls Tony Adams. This time he gets through, but a secretary answers and says that Mr. Adams is out of the office. That doesn't count, so James calls Ralph Bolsterood. He's in a meeting.

"This is boring," says Buster.

"No," I say. "This is real detective work."

"Well, it's not like in the movies," says Buster. "This would be the most boring movie in the world."

"In a movie this is the part they skip over," I explain. "You see Humphrey Bogart flip through the pages, make a face, and then start dialing. There's some music and you see the pages flip by, then—poof!—he's talking to Harvey Windbag, the very guy he's looking for!"

Buster doesn't look impressed. "Do you guys want to see my brother's magazines, instead? Mom got rid of the one she caught me reading, but he's got others and I know where he keeps them."

James and I look at each other. I sort of do and sort of don't. James looks like he feels the same way. But we both shake our heads at the same time. A mystery to solve is better than any magazine. Even one full of women in black underwear.

Finally, James reaches somebody who is at home. His name is Bob Desjardins. James tells him why he's calling. Bob says he'll keep it in mind and ask around.

Buster doesn't want a turn. He's making himself another sandwich. "The magazine is pretty good," he says. "There are stories, too, about savage killers and spies and . . . other stuff."

But now that we're off and running, we're not interested. I call six people but all I get is: "Flatley and Sons," or "Morgan, Morgan and Biggles," or "McCruddy's Stationery, how may I direct your call?"

"Which proves my point," says James. "If it were a woman's address book it wouldn't be full of men who were at the office."

Finally, I get someone on the line. And this time it *is* a woman.

"Could I speak to Nate Lavender, please?" I ask politely. There is an intake of air, but no reply.

"Hello?"

"There is no Nate Lavender at this number," says the woman hesitantly. Her voice sounds wary. "Who is this, please?"

I cover the mouthpiece. "She asked who it is," I whisper to James, who shakes his head at me. I remove my hand from the receiver. "Uh, no one," I say. "Just a friend." James is slashing his hand across his neck like I should hang up, but I don't want to. I like her voice.

"Please," she says. "Tell me who you are."

She sounds worried. I stutter a bit. "I . . . I must have the wrong number. Sorry."

"No," she says. "What do you want? Please!"

"Uh, thanks. Sorry to bother you. Goodbye." And I hang up as quickly as I can. But even as I place the receiver on its silver hook, I hear her voice demanding again to know who is calling. What did I hear? Suspicion? Fear?

I tell the others what she said. "That's weird," says Buster. "If there wasn't any Nate Lavender, why would she get so upset?"

"That's what I was thinking."

James has taken the address book back from me. "Twenty-nine Quigley Street," he says.

"Where is that?"

"Down near the stadium." He looks up from the address book and he doesn't have to say what's on his mind.

"Come on," I say. I push myself away from the table. "What are we waiting for?"

But Buster doesn't want to go. "It's too cold," he says. "I think I'll just hang around here . . . maybe do a little reading."

◎ ◎ ◎

So it's just James and I who make our way over to Quigley Street. The wind is behind us pushing us along like an impatient school yard monitor. It's dark. Luckily, it isn't too far. As we wait for the lights at Fifth and Bank, I point to the telephone booth.

"That's where I found it."

James gets this calculating look in his eye. "Funny phoning someone who only lives two blocks away," he says.

Number twenty-nine is a large old red brick house with a narrow front porch. The brickwork is cracked. The porch tips forward. There's a rusty iron railing on one side of the steps that looks pretty shaky. The steps need paint, and so does the front door. Through the window in the door we can see a light bulb dangling from a wire in the ceiling of the entranceway.

We walk by the house but there is nowhere to go. Quigley's a dead end. Almost. There's an alley off to the right, across the street. So we stand there, stamping our feet up and down to keep warm, watching number twenty-nine. Lights are on upstairs, but the curtains are drawn. We shiver and wait, not sure what to do next.

Then we see someone coming up the street, a chubby man in a khaki parka and a fur hat, which he holds down with one hand because the wind is so strong. He's holding a lunch pail in the other hand close to his chest like a tiny shield. He turns onto the path to twenty-nine and hurries up the steps.

The front door doesn't seem to be locked. He goes in and stops to collect his mail from one of the mailboxes on the wall. I didn't realize until now that the house is divided up into apartments.

Once the man is gone, we sneak back across the street and up the front walk. James tries the door. It opens.

There are four mailboxes, but only three apartment doors opening onto the entranceway. The linoleum floor is slick with muddy footprints. A striped umbrella sits outside the door to apartment 1A. The chubby man's galoshes sit outside 1B. On the mailboxes are printed the numbers: 1A, 1B, 2A (Back), and 2B. Below each number on a slip of paper is the name of the tenant. The tenant in apartment 2B is listed as L. Lavender.

"Bingo!" whispers James. "Should we knock?"

I think of the woman's voice, how nervous she sounded. I'm not sure. I look out the window. No one is coming. Then I notice the magazines and flyers lying on the shelf under the mailboxes. I sort through them. There is a magazine in a brown paper wrapper, still curled up with an elastic band around it. I pull off the elastic band and open it up. It's *Chatelaine*. I show it to James. His eyes almost bug out of his head. It's addressed to Natasha Lavender. *Natasha*?

I pull the little black book out of my pocket. *Nate* Lavender.

The plot thickens.

Just then we hear footsteps on a staircase—the stairs behind the door that says 2B! We push through the front door back out onto the porch.

"The magazine!" whispers James.

I'm still clutching *Chatelaine*. I dash back and throw it on the shelf. It wobbles and falls onto the sloppy wet floor. I go to pick it up but by now the footsteps are way too close. I slip out the door but not in time to run down the porch stairs without being seen.

I lean against the wall beside the front door. James is down hiding in the bushes. He puts his finger to his lips. "Shhhhhhh!" he says.

As if I need him to tell me!

After a moment, he nods at me. I know what he means—it's safe to peek.

There is a woman in the entranceway with her back to the door. She has white-blond shoulder-length hair flipped up at the bottom. She's looking at the mail she just took out of the box marked 2B.

The woman's hair gleams like a Breck Shampoo ad on the back of one of my sisters' magazines. It's lustrous—that's the only word for it.

She bends over and picks up the magazine. She holds it at arm's length. It's dripping wet. Suddenly, she starts to turn toward the front door and I pull my head back.

I hold my breath, ready to scram if she comes to the door. She doesn't.

After a while, James nods the all-clear but he mouths the word "careful."

She is still standing in the middle of the entranceway, facing me now, but looking down. She is frowning and there is something funny about her frown, something about her lips, but I can't figure out what. Her hair is perfect and her face is pretty but she sure is not happy.

"Natasha?"

It's a man's voice coming from the stairway.

She glances toward the open door to apartment 2B and wraps her arms around her chest.

She is all in white. White high heels, white pleated skirt, white angora sweater, and a wide white belt. She even wears white bangles on her wrist. The only color is her lipstick and her nails, which are as red as blood.

The Woman in White.

"Natasha, what the hell are you doing?"

She sighs. Her mouth opens as if she is going to say something. But she shuts it quick. Then she turns her head toward the staircase.

"Coming," she says. "I'll be right up."

But she doesn't move. She looks back toward the front door and again I pull my head away and hold my breath. I plaster myself against the cold bricks. Next thing I know she's at the window. If she turned her head even a *tiny* bit to the left she would see me, but she doesn't.

There's a little hitch in her upper lip; the two parts don't meet properly. She looks helpless. I almost want her to see me now. I want to apologize for phoning and upsetting her. It seems that's all I do these days. First I upset Dad, then my teacher, and now this beautiful woman.

I want to give her the address book, even if it isn't hers. I wish I'd never found it. Her breath fogs up the glass. Her face goes out of focus, kind of dreamy-looking. Then a voice cries from above.

"For God's sake, woman!"

And Natasha Lavender closes her eyes. Her long lashes rest on her high white cheekbones. Then she turns to go.

I hurry to the window to see her one more time. She pulls the door to apartment 2B closed behind her and I hear her footsteps climb the stairs.

I realize that I'm holding my breath. I reach up to touch the glass where the mist from her breath still lingers. I want to write something in the vapor. I don't know what. I reach up to touch it. But the vapor is on the other side.

A FIGHT IN THE NIGHT

Whiplash is on at seven-thirty, but I don't watch it. My mind is so full I don't think there is any room up there, not even for cowboys. I go to my room and sit at my desk. My desk is under the gable right in front of the window, but I can't see anything except a reflection of my room and me in the glass. We're both kind of a mess.

I can't see what's happening outside but I can hear it, all right. I'm sitting tucked between sloping walls like a Plains Cree in a tepee, with the winter wind prowling around outside like a pack of wolves.

I want to write down the minutes of our class meeting. Not the official minutes. I want to write down everything that happened while it's still clear in my memory. I don't exactly know why but I don't want it inside me—I want to get it out. Like when the Indian scout sucks the poison out of a rattlesnake bite.

The thing is, I can't write because of the Woman in

White. I can't get her out of my head. I keep seeing her face looking out of the window into the late afternoon darkness.

Natasha Lavender.

I can't forget her face framed by her hair-commercial hair. She looked abandoned, like a woman in a horror movie when she realizes that her friends have all been turned into zombie pod people.

There was something else about Natasha Lavender's face. I go downstairs and find Letitia in her room. She's looking through some sheet music, just about to start singing scales.

"What is it, Rex?"

I describe Natasha's mouth, the way her upper lip kind of jogged in the middle.

"That's called a harelip," she says.

"Even if there isn't any hair on it?"

"Not that kind of hair," she says. "The other hare—like a rabbit."

I think about the Woman in White. Her face didn't look like a rabbit's. Her face was beautiful, with big sad brown eyes.

"I think harelip isn't the polite word for it," says Letitia. "I think it's called a cleft lip. Do you know someone with one?" I shake my head. "It might hurt a person's feelings if you call it a harelip," she adds. I thank her and leave in a kind of a daze.

I finally manage to get writing. I try to remember everything that happened in the classroom that afternoon in the order it happened. That's all I want to do, make a list: this, then this, then this. I don't want to miss anything. It feels important. Like Perry Mason with a big court case, I want to have my facts straight.

When I stop writing, I've filled seven pages. I feel a bit better. I look up. There I am in the window. I wave. But something has changed. I look closer. The wind has stopped—that's it. The howling, prowling wolves have moved off. I stare at the window—try to see through the reflection of my messy room and me. There *is* something going on outside.

Can it really be true?

I jump out of my chair and run to turn off the light and close the door. Then I race back to my desk, sit down, and look out the window, which is now almost free of reflections.

Snow!

I feel tingly inside and at the same time I feel calm. I stand up and look down onto Clemow Avenue. The ground is already covered. The snow glitters under the streetlight.

How long have I been writing—a month? I look at the luminous hands of my bedside clock. It's nine-thirty.

"Rex?"

I turn in my chair. It's my mother. She's standing at the door silhouetted by the landing light.

"What are you doing sitting in the dark?" she asks. She doesn't sound angry. "May I turn on the light?"

"Sure. I was just watching the snow."

"Indeed," she says.

She flips on the light. I blink, look at her, and blink again.

She's wearing a dress. My mother is wearing a dress! Well, actually, she always wears dresses, but this is a party kind of dress. It's made of some shimmery material with sparkles in it and the skirt is full as if she's wearing crinolines. My sisters wear crinolines to make their skirts look like hot air balloons. But I've never seen my mum in one. And her hair is done up and she's wearing pearls and high heels.

"What's going on?"

"Your father and I are going out."

"Just you two?"

She chuckles. "Yes, silly. Come on now, get into your pajamas."

I get up and take my pjs from the end of the bed. I start to undress, then stop myself.

"Mum, I'm eleven, you know."

She covers her eyes. I change in a big hurry and hop under the covers.

"Where are you going?" I ask.

"Oh, a movie, I suspect."

"*Mutiny on the Bounty*?"

"Maybe."

"*Rio Bravo* is still on."

She laughs again. "We might end up just going for a drink."

I lay my head down. My pillow is frosty cold and the shock wakes me up. This is getting stranger and stranger. There's a liquor cabinet in the dining room with all kinds of drinks in it. Why do they need to go out?

"Aren't you worried about the snow? It might be slippery." My parents don't go *out*. Something must be wrong.

"Come on now," she says, tucking me in. "Enough questions."

She bends down to give me a kiss and a hug. She doesn't even make me go and brush my teeth. And, as if that weren't enough, she's wearing perfume. This is serious.

She sits on the edge of my bed and strokes my hair. "Yesterday," she says, "when you missed going with your father to the Armistice Day ceremony, did he talk to you about anything in particular?"

"He told me a story."

"What kind of a story?"

I scratch my head. Even though it was only yesterday, it seems like a million years ago. So much has happened. Trying to remember it is like looking for something in the closet. I have to throw out all these boots and tennis shoes and galoshes. Ah! There it is.

"It was about cheese," I say. "And this . . ." But I don't want to talk about the German sniper.

"And this what?" she asks.

"About this soldier getting blown up by a hand grenade."

Her hand rests on my arm. "Nothing else?" she says.

"No. Why?"

She sits another moment and then sighs and gets to her feet. "Sleep tight, darling," she says. I'm usually allowed to read for a while, but I don't bother mentioning it. She leaves the door a little bit open. I listen to her high heels click, click, click slowly down the stairs.

What was that about?

I jump out of bed and go to my window. Eventually, I see them below, Mum and Dad, walking carefully down the front steps to the path. Mum is hanging on to his arm, really tightly. Then they stop. Dad is looking up at the snow. Mum does, too, but then she shudders. Even in her mink coat she's cold. She lets go of his arm and heads toward the car, walking carefully through the snow in her high heels. Dad just stands there looking up at the sky or the trees or something. I hear the car door open and close.

Dad doesn't move. After about a million heartbeats, the car door opens again. Mum says something, I guess, because Dad looks toward the car. Then her door closes again, harder this time. Finally, Dad walks toward the car, his head bent low, his hands deep in his pockets.

Another mystery.

There're too many of them to think about. I jump back into bed shivering and lie there listening to the snow. You can't hear it but it's there, and it's comforting, somehow. All these mysteries to solve, like a bunch of toys left out in the garden all getting covered up so you can't see them anymore.

◎ ◎ ◎

I'm not sure what wakes me up. I look at my clock. It's after eleven. I listen again.

Voices.

Mum and Dad?

Then somebody runs up the main staircase to the second floor. A second somebody runs after the first somebody. Now somebody is running back down the stairs. More voices. I throw back my covers and climb out of bed. I look out the window. Snow has piled up along the sill. The car isn't back yet.

I go to the top of the attic stairs and listen. I hear low voices arguing. Creeping down the stairs and peering over the railing, I can just make out Cassiopeia and Annie Oakley halfway up the main staircase below.

"I was not," says Annie.

"Yes, you were!" says Cassiopeia.

"Prove it," says Annie.

"Your bedtime was ten-thirty and I found you in the study. You were snooping and I'm telling Daddy."

Annie is holding on to the railing with both hands,

probably trying to stop herself from wringing Cassie's neck. She's in her cowboy pajamas with the lariats, cactuses, and rattlers on them. Cassie is all dressed up as if Mr. Odsburg might be dropping by any minute.

And then a strange thing happens. When I think about it later, back in bed, I'm sure I must have telepathic powers because Annie starts to laugh as if she knew exactly what I was thinking.

"Stop that!" says Cassie. "You sound like a lunatic."

"I'm *not* a lunatic. And if you tell Daddy I was snooping, I'll tell him about you and Mr. Odsburg."

I have to clap my hand over my mouth to stop from whooping with laughter.

"What is that supposed to mean?" says Cassie, but you can tell from her voice she's going to back off.

"About what you were doing," says Annie.

"We weren't doing . . ."

Cassiopeia stops and in the silence I hear what she is hearing: the car pulling into the driveway. I scoot back to bed and my warring sisters split up: Cassie down the stairs, Annie up to bed. I listen but there are no more angry words. No one hurries up to Annie's room to give her what for. The fight is over and all that's left is another mystery.

What was Annie doing in Daddy's study after her bedtime? I try to count up all the mysteries, but the other ones are now completely buried in snow and I fall asleep trying to find them.

SPEED BONNIE BOAT

When I wake up the next morning I make a list before my brain knows what's happening. I feel smart, just like the Scarecrow in *The Wizard of Oz* when the wizard gives him a diploma. Morning is like a diploma.

I sit at my desk, my teeth chattering from the morning cold, writing out all the mysteries in my life:

1. Why has my father been acting so strange?
2. What is the story my mother thought he was going to tell me on Armistice Day?
3. Why was Annie snooping in Dad's study?
4. Who is the beautiful Natasha Lavender and why is she so sad?
5. Why is she called "Nate" in some guy's address book?
6. What is Kathy going to do about Doctor Arnold Schwartz?

7. What is my class going to do about Miss Garr?

Phew! That's a lot of questions.

Now I allow myself to look out the window. I didn't want to look until I'd made the list because I was sure my brain would explode.

Boom!

It explodes.

My head has nothing in it but snow. Everything is white except for the tire tracks on the street. There are tire tracks leaving our driveway, so Dad has already gone to work.

The sun's not quite up yet, but there isn't a cloud in the sky and everything is sparkling. I think of my friends back in Vancouver walking to school in the rain.

Ha ha ha.

When I get downstairs to the kitchen, I can't talk to Mum because she's too busy with breakfast, and I can't talk to Annie because Mum is there. I don't want to get anyone else in trouble. Besides, Annie hardly notices me. She is too busy watching Cassie dabbing teensy specks of Marmite on little triangles of dry toast. Marmite is this stuff English people eat that looks like tar smeared on the bottom of your shoe. Annie is watching Cassie like a rattlesnake at a gopher's hole. She's got her hands in her lap and I bet she's got a weapon there. If Cassie says one word about last night, it will be the last thing she ever says.

But who cares!

All I really want to do is get out into that snow. I eat my breakfast quickly because I have a feeling it's going to take a while to get my winter gear on. Mum bought everything at the Hadassah Bazaar. I lay it all out on the floor in the living room: a big fat quilted bright blue snow jacket with a hood, fat black snow pants, mitts, heavy socks, boots, a scarf, and a Toronto Maple Leafs bobble hat, except they call them toques here. I already have on a turtleneck sweater that Mum knitted for me. It's white with black spots. I look just like a dalmatian.

I've heard stories about people freezing to death and I'm not taking any chances.

Mum decides to be funny.

"Rex? Rex, where are you?"

I laugh but she can't hear me because my scarf is wrapped eighteen times around my mouth. She has to open the door for me and I step out like a zombie pod person. It's the morning of the living dead.

The sun is up and it's so bright, bouncing off the snow, I can't see a thing. I clump down the stairs to the path and turn west on Clemow. Now the sun is behind me and I can see what I was already beginning to guess, because I'm sweltering inside my winter clothes.

The snow is melting.

In the time it took me to eat a bowl of Cheerios and get dressed, winter is almost over. I turn and waddle back home and take off just about everything. I head out again with just my toque and my dalmatian sweater on.

In class, Miss Garr is as nice as can be. You'd think yesterday never happened. I stare at her whenever she's not looking my way, wondering if maybe she isn't Miss Garr but her twin sister—the nice one who the other Miss Garr usually has tied up in the basement.

She doesn't even look so bad. She's wearing an apple green suit with a dragon's blood red blouse under it. She has a pink ribbon in her hair, which clashes but makes her look young.

We have art this morning and we are supposed to draw animals for a poster contest sponsored by the SPCA, which Buster thinks stands for the Society for the Presumption of Cruelty to Animals. I'm doing three Canada geese flying through the clouds, with the caption "Don't Shoot Me!" It's a pretty good poster. Looking around me, I think I've got an excellent chance of winning. Kathy is drawing a squirrel that's been run over by a car. Sami is drawing a bear caught in a leghold trap. His page is covered with blood. Rhonda, who sits in front of me, is drawing a kitten, except it looks more like a toy than a real kitten. Her caption is "Wouldn't You Like to Take Me Home for Christmas?" which is pretty barfy and not about cruelty. Except having to live at Rhonda's would be cruel.

I'm working away at the honkers when suddenly Miss Garr is standing beside me. She's got her hands on her knees and she's bending down so that she can look closely.

"Well done," she says.

Whatever my part was in yesterday's meltdown, she seems to have forgiven me.

"Thanks," I mutter. But I haven't forgiven her.

Then she bends closer and whispers directly in my ear. "Do you know what I think, Rex?" she says, her voice full of happy surprise. "I think we all could do with a little song."

Oh no!

I look at my picture. "I was just working on the eyes," I say very quietly, so it doesn't sound like I'm arguing.

"And the eyes are very good, very good indeed. You are a very talented artist. But it would make the whole exercise so much more enjoyable for the class, don't you think, if you sang us something? How about 'Speed Bonnie Boat'?"

No! Not "Speed Bonnie Boat"!

I clear my throat. "Actually, I think I caught a chill on the way here this morning."

Miss Garr laughs in a tinkly way. "Now, now," she says. "You can't fool me." Then she leans in close so her lips almost touch my ear. "You don't want to let your classmates down, do you?"

It isn't really a question. I think for just a moment whether it would be worth saying no and getting the strap. I stare one last time at the three geese. "Don't Shoot Me!" Then I sigh and lay my pencil carefully in the trough at the top of my desk.

"Class," says Miss Garr, clapping her hands three times. "Rex has volunteered to sing us a song to help us along with our artistic endeavors."

My face goes bright red. Beet red.

"Come along now, Rex. How about 'Speed, Bonnie Boat'?"

"Speed, Bonnie Boat." About two days after Miss Garr took over our class, I put up my hand when she asked if anyone knew that song. Her favorite song. How was I to know she would make me sing it? How was I to know she would make me sing it again?

I stand in the center of the classroom with my hands folded in front of me. Where is the guy to put on the blindfold? Where is the firing squad?

"Now, Rex," she says. "Don't be shy."

I look out at the class. They're all looking down at their desks, except for Randy Mooney who is sneering at me and Tanya McCurdy who is rolling her eyes and Polly who is frowning as if I'm a traitor. It's so unfair! I glance over at Donnie. Does he think I'm a traitor? Donnie's looking out the window.

"We're waiting, Rex," says Miss Garr, and her voice isn't

as sweet as it was a minute ago. Soon she'll be looking for rocks.

Frantically, I look over at Kathy Brown who is staring right at me. Her eyes seem to say, "It's okay. We know it wasn't your idea."

Oh, well. Might as well get it over.

Speed, bonnie boat, like a bird on the wing,
Onward! the sailor's cry.
Carry the lad that was born to be king,
Over the seas to Skye.

And then the bell rings. Just one verse too late.

I go straight home at the end of the day. I don't wait for the others. Mum is in the kitchen having a cup of tea. The Sausage is sitting in his high chair having a cup of fairy tea. That's tea with mostly milk and sugar in it. Dinah Shore is singing a cheery song about "courtin' in the mornin' " but it doesn't cheer me up.

"What did you do at school today?" asks Mum.

"Miss Garr made me dance on her desk with no clothes on."

"Not even your socks?" says Mum. "That can't be hygienic."

The Sausage looks terrified.

"Don't worry, dear," says Mum, patting his chubby little hand.

"She should be fired," I say. "She should be electrocuted."

Then Mum pats my hand as well. "I once had a teacher I thought should be boiled in oil. Other students wanted her hung by her toes or buried in the desert and eaten by fire ants, and still others thought she should be fed to crocodiles. We could never agree on the best torture and, alas, I think she lived to be a hundred and eighty."

I don't feel like joking. I wander off to the living room and curl up in the settee under the front window. That's what we call it, a settee. Nobody else in Canada has a settee. They have couches.

I look out at the already dark sky. I wish the winter hadn't taken off like a scaredy-cat. It's gone. There isn't a flake of white out there.

There are newspapers in a basket beside the settee. On the top is a picture of Santa on a rocket ship at a department store downtown on Saturday. Big deal. I look at the next page.

There's a picture from Armistice Day. Madame Vitaline Lanteigne from New Brunswick laying a wreath on behalf of all the mothers of Canada. She had five sons: three of them were killed in World War II; the other two were wounded. Five kids—almost the same as my family.

I try to imagine Cassie, Letitia, and Annie—all dead. "Have you got any more, Mrs. Norton-Norton? Ah, good. Off you go, Rex and Flora Bella. Oops! Sorry about that. We'll just dig those bullets out and you'll be good as new!"

No wonder Dad gets depressed around this time of year.

TWO BIRDS
WITH ONE STONE

Luckily, I wake up the next morning invisible. This happens to me from time to time. I wish I could take better advantage of it: sneak into movie theatres for free, steal candy from the corner store, write things behind Miss Garr's back on the blackboard. But it isn't the *good* kind of invisibility. I just *feel* invisible. I still have to show up where I'm supposed to be. So I go to school and I go to lunch and I walk home with my friends.

This kind of invisibility works best if you don't say anything. Someone cracks a joke in class—you don't laugh. Someone asks you a question—you don't answer. You mind your own business. Someone needs help—you don't do anything at all.

◎ ◎ ◎

The next week, the weather turns completely mild. Winter gives up without even a fight! In the school yard, out comes the peewee football again, and the guys choose up sides.

"Were you away?" says Buster.

See what I mean?

"You going to play?" says James.

"Maybe." I still feel only half here. I look around and see Donnie Dangerfield leaning against the fence. "You want to play?"

He holds up his left palm. The blisters are mostly gone. For the first couple of days after he got the strap his fingers looked like boiled frankfurters.

"What did your parents say?"

He shrugs. "My dad said, 'That'll teach you not to be such a smart-ass.' And my mom said, 'Jesus H. Christ, so I gotta do the dishes?' "

I wish I hadn't asked. I'm not sure what my parents would do, but Annie Oakley would have been down here in a flash to scalp Miss Garr.

"Are you coming, Rex?"

"Start without me," I shout. I look at Donnie to see if he minds me hanging around. He just shrugs some more. He looks a little invisible himself.

I lean against the fence. I can't think of anything to say. Being visible again suddenly seems like way too much work. Then Donnie looks at me and there's this little worm of a grin sitting on the edge of his mouth.

"What are the words to that song you like to sing?"

"I do *not* like to sing it."

"Sure you do," he says, poking me with his elbow. I know he's kidding. I poke him back. "Seriously," he says, "what are the words?"

Finally, I recite them to him. I didn't use to hate the song, but now I do. He repeats them after me. He remembers the tune pretty well and hums it through.

"Who's the lad that's born to be king?" he asks.

"Bonnie Prince Charlie."

He screws up his face. "Bonnie is a girl's name."

He sings it again. He's got a good voice.

"Got it," he says. Then there's that worm of a grin again, like bait dancing on a hook. "Next time she does that to you, I'll join in, okay?"

I feel as if someone just gave me a present and it isn't even my birthday. "You'll get in trouble."

He shrugs. "I know. But if everybody learned the words . . ."

He leaves the idea dangling in the air between us.

As if he can tell something is up, Zoltan comes over to join us. He usually stands by himself at recess, watching everything, listening. We tell him Donnie's plan. He nods. He pokes me in the chest.

"You write out words to song," he says. He pokes himself in the chest. "I learn them. Wait and see." Then he grins. "I have bad, bad voice."

We all laugh.

"Look at her," says Zoltan. He nods his head toward the playground where Miss Garr is on yard duty. She's helping some little tyke climb the stairs of the slide. Another first-grader is leaning against her leg.

"She got wrong class," says Zoltan.

It's true. The little kids seem to like Miss Garr. Then I remember what she said to me, back when she first arrived.

"She doesn't like it when people grow up," I say.

"Tough," says Donnie. "What's she going to do about it?"

Zoltan shakes his head. "When she make you sing, it same like the other day. You know, when she pretend Donnie say you are stupid."

"How is it the same?"

His brow wrinkles. He is concentrating hard. "How you say she make word come out of you, you don't want?"

"She puts words in your mouth," I say.

"Yes," he says, snapping his fingers. "She puts words in Donnie's mouth. She puts words in your mouth—says you want to sing when you don't want to sing. The same thing, yes?"

"Yes." He's right. It *is* the same thing. And I'm kind of amazed. When Zoltan arrived at school, he hardly knew a word of English. How could you learn anything when you couldn't understand the teacher? I thought. The thing is, he does understand her. He understands her really well.

He shakes his head again. "My father is newspaper writer. How do you say . . . ?" He types in the air.

"A journalist?"

"Yes. Journalist. Back in Budapest. He support the revolution in '56. Write about in paper. Taking back our country from Communists." Zoltan smashes his fist into his palm. "Yes! Good!" Then he drops his hands to his sides. "But Soviets crush revolution. My father? He go to jail. They say he is enemy of country. In their own newspaper, they make up lies. They put words in his mouth."

"Is your dad still in jail?"

Zoltan shakes his head. "My father get us out of country. Come here. We lucky. Premier Nagy? Not so lucky. He try to make the revolution? They execute him." Zoltan makes gunshot sounds. Three of them.

He nods toward Miss Garr. She is kneeling to tie a little kid's boot. Another kid comes up to ask her something. Miss Garr laughs. The kid laughs, too.

"Maybe older kids are too hard for her to figure out," I say. "I mean, tying somebody's shoelace is easy. Putting a kid on a slide is easy. Maybe we're too complicated for her."

"Yeah," says Donnie. "We're real complicated. You know why?"

I shake my head.

"Because we know the words to the song," he says. Then he starts singing "Speed Bonnie Boat" in a lusty voice. Zoltan joins in and gets me to sing, too. Now all three of us are singing it together.

I glance over toward Miss Garr. She's staring at me and

looks disappointed. I'm getting good at disappointing people.

◎ ◎ ◎

After school, I meet up with James and Buster and Kathy.

"We've got some bad news," says Buster. "Tell him, Kathy."

Kathy frowns and the clear sky blue of her eyes is suddenly full of lightning. "I was out Sunday for a bit and when I got home, Dr. Arnold was there."

"Tell him what they were doing," says Buster.

She makes a face as if she just bit into an oyster.

"Were they kissing?"

"Worse," says James.

I don't want to think about what would be worse. Luckily, Kathy doesn't make me guess.

"They were reading *Better Homes and Gardens* magazine."

I feel as if I've missed something. Then James draws a rectangle in the air. A house?

"Holy moly. They're talking about building a house?"

Kathy looks grumpy. "Not exactly. But they were talking about what they liked and didn't like. 'Oh, I like French doors.' 'You do? So do I.' 'What do you think of Formica countertops?' 'Oh, oh, oh, I love Formica countertops.' It was disgusting."

"Things are moving fast," I say.

"It stinks!" says Kathy, throwing her hands up in the air. "Mom and I had everything worked out. And now there's Mom and me *and* Dr. Arnold *and* little Missy."

I almost tell her that she still only has *half* the family I have, but she isn't finished.

"Why did he have to fall in love with her? Why, why, why? There must be lots of women who'd just love to marry a nice doctor."

We all shake our heads sympathetically.

"Too bad he didn't fall in love with Miss Garr," I say.

"Impossible," says Kathy.

"It would be so perfect," I say. "It would kill two birds with one stone. They'd probably elope and you'd get your mother back and we'd get a new teacher."

"But who'd ever want to marry Miss Garr?" says Buster. "She's the Bride of Frankenstein."

"She's not so bad-looking," I say. The others gag. "No, I mean, really. Not all the time. And she can be nice as long as you're only about three feet high."

"I know," says Kathy. "I watched her pushing Missy in the swing. Missy was as happy as a clam."

Kathy is not as happy as a clam, that's for sure. And I'd really like to make her happy. In a fairy tale it would be a cinch. Just sprinkle a little fairy dust and—poof!—Dr. Arnold's in love with Miss Garr.

Wait a minute! It *is* possible. Not that I've got any fairy dust, but . . .

"Rex, are you all right?"

The others are looking at me. "Maybe it's not too late," I say.

"Not too late for what?" says Buster.

"Not too late for Dr. Arnold and Miss Garr to fall in love."

◎ ◎ ◎

"This is crazy," says James.

"No it's not," I say. We're all at Buster's, sitting in the kitchen drinking Vernors Ginger Ale and eating Cheezies.

"Here's my plan so far. We write a love letter to Miss Garr from Dr. Arnold."

"Why not the other way around?" says Buster.

"Because girls fall in love way more easily than guys," I say. "Believe me, I know."

Buster looks confused. "Then why don't we write a letter from Miss Garr to Dr. Arnold if she's the one who's fallen in love?"

Kathy shakes her head. "Look," she says. "No girl would write to a guy and say she's in love with him. He would think she was a tramp. But if a guy—a doctor guy—writes to a lonely woman, she would fall in love with him right on the spot."

"Exactly!" I say.

"It's nuts," says James, tugging on his gray patch. "As

soon as she talks to him she'll find out that he didn't write the letter."

I hadn't thought that far. Everybody takes long slow sips of their Vernors.

"Anyway," says James. "You can't make someone fall in love."

"Of course not," says Kathy. "But she'd probably act all sweet and friendly to him, if she *thought* he was in love with her. He likes to pick up Missy at school. If Miss Garr thought he liked her, she'd wear nice clothes and say how nice Missy is. He'll notice her, at least. And maybe, by the time she finds out he didn't write the letter, they will already be in love."

Kathy beams at me as if I just invented a miracle cure.

"It could work," I say.

James frowns. "I don't know. She might think he's just weird. And how are *we* going to write a love letter anyway?"

That's when it comes to me—an even *better* plan. "We'll send a letter from a friend. An anonymous friend. Someone who knows Dr. Arnold and knows how he is yearning for Miss Garr."

"But how do we make it look like an adult?"

"I'll type it," I say. "I know how to type."

Kathy looks hopeful.

I'm on a roll. "Maybe the letter is from an expert, like Dear Abby," I say. "Or Ann Landers."

Now even James looks a little less skeptical.

Then it comes to me in a flash. "Dr. Love."

"Huh?"

"Dr. Love. Like in girls' magazines. There're always these columns."

"What kind of columns?" asks Buster.

"Advice to the lovelorn, you know. Girls write in because they're in love with someone and he's cheating on them or doesn't know they exist and they don't know what to do."

Kathy laughs out loud. "Perfect!" she says. "Then when Dr. Arnold says he doesn't know what Miss Garr is talking about, she'll just think he's being shy. You could even say something like that in the letter."

They're all looking at me.

"Are you up for it?" says James.

I'm not sure. But it would be a great trick. And if there was anyone in the world who deserved a trick played on her . . .

"Oh, please," says Kathy. "I mean, even if it doesn't work, at least Dr. Arnold will think twice, right? He'll think, 'Hey, there's this other woman who likes me. Maybe there are lots of other women who like me, so why should I marry Mary Brown?' You see what I mean?"

"If there is anyone who could do it, it would be you," says James.

I blush. I am pretty good with words.

"Well, I could give it a try."

Kathy jumps out of her chair and gives me a hug. Whoa! She's never done that before.

"I know you can do it," she says.

"Of course he can do it," says Buster. "He's Dr. Looooove!"

DR. LOVE

When I get home, Mum asks me if I'll take the Sausage out for a walk.

"I can't," I tell her. "I'm Dr. Love."

I gather a bunch of my sisters' magazines, *Glamour*, *Seventeen*, *Mademoiselle*—a big stack—and haul them up to my room. Then I look for the lovelorn columns. The letters are always signed "Please help me" or "Worried" or "Sleepless."

I have to scrunch up my nose to read this stuff. There are a lot of unhappy people in the world. I read six or seven to get a feel for it and I just end up feeling crazy. If dating and marriage are going to be this difficult, maybe I'll stay a bachelor.

Then I think about Kathy hugging me and I have to get on with it. But my brain starts playing tricks on me, because the next minute I'm thinking about Natasha Lavender and how sad she looked. I see her all dressed in white, making the cold glass of her front door fog up with her breath. I see her chest rising and falling, rising and falling under her angora sweater.

I write the letter in pencil first. I get the dictionary from my father's office and the thesaurus, too. This is something most kids my age don't even know about. It's this book with synonyms in it—words that mean the same thing as other words. My sisters use it all the time.

"This butter is far too oleaginous."

"I think Pat Boone is resplendent."

"I'm going to eviscerate you."

It's in the thesaurus that I find the words "humanitarian" and "amorous." I was just going to say kind and loving but a doctor would use bigger words. There are lots of big words in the thesaurus: infirmity, tragically, magnetized—really good words.

It takes a long time to get it right, but finally I'm ready.

Dear Miss Garr,

You don't know me but over the last few weeks I herd a lot about you. Why just the other day my good friend Dr. Arnold Schwartz mentioned your name. He was picking up his daughter Missy and he saw you their helping out and smiling at all the little children. Dr. Schwarts thinks you are a very humanitarian and amorous person. I ought to know. I am also a doctor. When I hear a pasient talk the way Dr. Arnold talks I know what the infirmity is! Tragically Missys mother left Dr. Arnold many years ago. Missy so misses having a mother. There is nothing like a woman's touch to make for a happy home. I hope you will not think it uncouth of me to interfere like this, but for my good friend Dr. Arnold's sake I hop you will consider having a chat with him. He is quiet shy. He may pretend to not know what you are talking about but beleive me he is very magnetized to you and he is a very nice and plesant and sucessful man. Maybe you to could go out for a drink or to the movies? I notice that Mutany on the Bounty is still playing at the Regent. What do you think? Remember, he may be bashful but as his doctor I can tell you there is only one cure. You know what I mean.

Yours very truly,
Dr. Love

I'm pretty proud of it. But by the time I'm done reading it over, it's dinnertime. After dinner, Letitia gets dibs on the typewriter for an essay for school. The final version of Dr. Love's letter will have to wait.

The next day Kathy arrives at school with an address for Miss Garr. There were only two Garrs in the phone book, Thomas and P.

"Bet it stands for Prune-Face," says Buster.

Everyone is impressed with my letter. James notices I spelled "patient" wrong and left the "e" off the word "hope," but otherwise everybody agrees it's perfect.

"Just what the doctor ordered," says Kathy. And we all laugh.

As soon as I get home, I go to type out the letter in Dad's study. I push through the door without knocking and there's Annie Oakley.

"What are you doing here?" she demands.

I'm backing out the door apologizing when I stop.

"What are *you* doing here?" I ask. "And why are you going through Dad's filing cabinet?"

"It's none of your business," she says. "Close the door."

I close the door. "Okay," I say. "So you won't mind if I tell him?"

She glares at me but I stand my ground. Our eyes lock. There we are, Godzilla and King Kong fighting over who gets to destroy Tokyo.

Finally, she slams the drawer shut. I've won!

"What's up?" I ask.

She scowls, but I can see that flicker of excitement in her eye. She's onto something.

"Remember that time I snuck up on Dad and he started talking in his sleep?"

"In German."

"Right. Well, one day last week, I came in without knocking and he was reading something at his desk. He covered it up the second he saw me."

She is speaking so quietly, I have to cross the room to hear her.

"Did you see it?"

She nods. "Just a corner of it. It was a letter written on that thin blue paper."

"Like the letters Mum and Dad get from England?"

"Like that," she says, "But this letter wasn't from England. It was from Germany."

I can't believe it. "How did you find out?"

"I pretended I was sad and needed a hug."

"Wasn't he suspicious?"

"Ha ha ha. Anyway, while he was giving me a hug, I managed to free one of my arms and shift the paper on his desk. The date at the top of the letter was . . ." She stops mid-sentence and goes to the desk, takes a pen, and writes on a scrap of paper:

8.11.46

Numbers. "Is it a code?"

"No, you nincompoop. The eighth of November, *nineteen-forty-six*."

Whoa. "That was just after the war."

"Right. But there was more . . ."

Dramatically, she picks up the pen again and writes:

Mein Liebchen

She writes it funny but I get what she's trying to do. She's making it look like old-fashioned German script.

"What does it mean?"

She puts the pen carefully back in the old mug, which is full of mechanical pencils and pens and a letter opener shaped like a dagger. She looks solemnly at me. "I think it means 'My darling.'"

I have to sit down.

My darling.

Finally, I look up at Annie. She has this expression on her face as if I'm going to call her a liar. Her fists are clenched. She's waiting to beat me up.

"I know someone at school who takes German," she says. "She said she would translate the letter for me if I could find it."

I glance at her. She's chewing her lip. Our eyes meet. She looks anxious. And then she says something I've never ever heard her say before.

"Maybe I was wrong."

I still don't speak and neither does she. Then before I know it, she marches out of the study and closes the door behind her.

I don't know what to think. Maybe she *is* wrong. Maybe *Mein Liebchen* means Mister Engineer.

After a while, I decide that if I'm going to type the letter I came in here to type, I'd better get to it. I find some of my father's best creamy-colored stationery and roll it into the typewriter.

Mum used to be a typist for a steamship company in Liverpool. She showed me how to type a letter properly so that I could thank my grandparents back in England for sending me Christmas presents, and impress them with how successful we are now that we live in Canada. I even know how to type an envelope.

I like typing. I'm really slow but it doesn't matter; it still looks impressive when you're finished. Nobody will ever guess that Dr. Love is only eleven years old.

I concentrate. Try to block all the funny thoughts that are circling around in my brain. It's kind of like a football game up there and these ferocious thoughts are blitzing the quarterback. You can block some of them but you can't get them all, and then—*Bam!*—you get blindsided.

Mein Liebchen—*Bam!*—Natasha Lavender—*Bam! Bam!* Once I start thinking of her, I can't stop. She sounded scared on the phone and yet hopeful, too.

Who are you? What do you want?

Then when I saw her, she looked so sad. I can still see her face. Her beautiful face, her big brown eyes, even her cleft lip.

Somehow, with all this on my mind, I get the letter typed. I look at the time on the mantel clock. Dad won't be home for another fifteen minutes. I seal up the letter to Miss Garr.

Then, just as I'm about to leave, I stare at the telephone as if it's a loaded gun.

Why not? I pull the little black book from my pocket. I take a deep breath and dial the number.

I hope she's home. I hope she's home.

"Yeah, who is it?"

It's a man.

"Hey, who is this?"

Any bets it's the guy who called down the stairs when Natasha was getting the mail.

"It's you, isn't it?" he says, his voice low and mean. I freeze. "You think I don't know about you?"

I couldn't speak now if I wanted to.

"What do you take me for, a chump?"

I should hang up but it's as if the receiver is glued to my ear.

"You are going to be sorry, buddy," he snarls. "You are going to wish you were never born. You hear me?"

With superhuman strength I wrestle the phone away from my ear and slam it down.

He knows me even though I didn't say a word. How could he?

I stare at the phone in terror, as if the cord is this long thin tunnel and right now Mr. Nasty L. Lavender is crawling along it all the way from Quigley Street, with a knife clenched between his teeth.

Then the study door swings open. I gasp, half expecting it to be him. But it's only Letitia, smiling.

"Din-din," she says cheerily. "And Cassiopeia has brought home Mr. Odsburg."

MR. ODSBURG

Cassiopeia thinks Mr. Odsburg's eyes are "scrummy," but I don't think she found that word in a thesaurus. Up close they just look bulgy to me. It's as if someone squeezed his neck too tight. They're a nice color, though, kind of greeny-blue like the ocean. His hair is the color of corn silk—almost white—and very soft-looking. Mr. Odsburg is very soft-looking all over.

"Are you the one who works in China?" asks Flora Bella, as soon as we're all seated.

"Well, yes," he says.

"That's a long way to go to work."

We all laugh except for Cassie, who closes her eyes.

"Pardon me?" says our guest, looking around. "Oh, yes. I see. Very funny."

"I know lots of jokes," says Flora Bella.

"Not now, dear," says Mum. "Gravy, Mr. Odsburg?"

"Uh, no, thank you very much."

"Actually Carl isn't in *china* any longer," says Cassie. "He has just been promoted, haven't you, Carl." He nods and she touches his hand.

"Good for you," says Dad. "And where exactly does a young man go when he's moving up from china?"

"Precious jewels."

"Carl is the new manager of precious jewels," says Cassie.

"Like diamonds?" says Letitia.

"Yes, diamonds," says Mr. Odsburg. "Diamonds, emeralds, sapphires."

"Lovely," says Mum. "When I was young, we had a cat named Opal."

"Mother," says Cassie. "Opals are only semiprecious."

"Well, she wasn't a very nice cat."

"Is that the one I ran over?" asks Dad.

Mum stops serving the lamb roast for a moment and then smiles. "Why, yes. I think it was. In the Austin?"

Dad nods. "Now, that, my man, was a real car."

Mr. Odsburg has a piece of potato almost to his mouth but he's forced to put it down in order to reply. "Yes, sir. I've heard good things about the Austin. They're difficult to buy here."

"More's the pity," says Dad.

"Carl has a Nash," says Cassie.

"Have you tried Calmitol?" asks Mum. "It will take away the itch."

"A *Nash*, Mother. Not a rash."

"A 1952 Nash Rambler Country Club two-door hardtop," says Mr. Odsburg.

"I don't believe it!" says Annie Oakley, bringing her fists down on the table.

"It's true," says Cassie. "It's black, with a red interior."

"I'm not talking about that," says Annie. "Didn't any-body hear what Daddy said? He said he drove over a cat." She glares at Mum. "When I shot the neighbor's cat, you took away my bow and arrow for two weeks."

"Yes, dear," says Mum. "But your father didn't *mean* to run over Opal and you *did* mean to shoot the neighbor's cat."

"I didn't hurt it," says Annie. "Those arrows are rub-bish."

The Sausage has been playing airplane with his string beans, but now he looks up fearfully. "Annie wants to shoot an apple off my head."

"Like William Tell!" says Letitia. Then she leans forward to get Mr. Odsburg's attention. Her heart-shaped locket ends up in her beans but she doesn't notice. "I can play the William Tell Overture on my cheeks. Would you like to hear?"

She immediately starts pitter-patting on her cheeks with her fingers and the theme from *The Lone Ranger* comes galloping out of her mouth.

"Na na na, na na na, na na na, na, na!"

"No singing at the table," says Mum. "And, Annie, you are not to shoot *anything* off Rupert's head."

"Who's Rupert?" asks Flora Bella.

"Your little brother," says Cassie. "The Sausage."

"Oh, right!"

"Really, this family . . ."

"Mr. Odsburg!" says Mum in such a startled way that we all look at her and then at him. "You have no meat."

"Uh, well . . ."

"Carl is a vegetarian," says Cassie. "*We* are vegetarians."

Sure enough, Cassie's plate is meatless. But it's the first I've heard of it. She sure ate her share of bacon at breakfast last Sunday.

Flora Bella leans close to me and whispers in my ear.

"What's a vegetarian?"

"Someone from Vegetaria."

"Can I get you some Marmite and toast?" says Mum.

"No thanks."

"An egg?"

"Really, it's not a problem."

"How about some cheese?" She is already wiping her mouth with her napkin and getting to her feet. "I have some lovely Stilton."

"No, no!" cries Mr. Odsburg. "Please. Everything is just hunky-dory. Don't disturb yourself. I'm a light eater."

Flora Bella suddenly starts choking and Annie hits her so hard on the back, Flora Bella's barrette flies off into the gravy boat. Even Mr. Odsburg finds that funny.

"Children, children," says Dad. "Kindly contain your hilarity with a modicum of restraint."

When he says that we always laugh more. I'm glad to see him in a better mood. Then Flora Bella fishes out her barrette and puts it right back on her head so the gravy drips down her face. She is the queen of gravy!

Before anyone can stop her, she excuses herself from the table and runs out of the room. She's back in a minute with a light bulb, which she hands to Mr. Odsburg.

"Eat it," she says.

"Pardon me?"

Flora Bella puts one hand on her hip and looks at me with a can-you-believe-it expression.

"You said you were a light eater," I explain.

"Oh," he says weakly. "Another joke." He looks overcome.

Cassiopeia folds her hands quietly in her lap. She bows her head. "You see what I have to live with?" she says, but not in a theatrical way. She can be very theatrical, but this is more like a hopeless prayer.

Mr. Odsburg solemnly takes her hand. She manages a little smile just for him. I'm sitting right across the table and I watch them—study them like a science project.

While all around me plates are collected and the sherry

trifle is brought out and Letitia sings something from *The Music Man* and the Sausage complains because Annie is washing his face and hands too roughly with a facecloth and Dad is cleaning out his pipe and beginning to look sad and far away again, I watch my oldest sister and her boyfriend who used to work in china but has been promoted to precious jewels. And I realize something I've never actually realized before.

One day—one day soon—she's going to leave us.

THE WOMAN IN BLACK

I go out for a walk in the not quite winter night. There's so much going on, no one will notice I'm missing as long as I'm back by bedtime. I need to clear my head. I need to think.

I pause by the mailbox at the corner of Clemow and Bank with the letter to Miss Garr in my hand. I stand there so long I start to shiver. I should probably have checked it over one more time. But even if I found a mistake, I wouldn't want to type it again, so what's the point. I'm not sure I want to send it but I kind of have to now. I promised Kathy.

I hesitate one long, last time.

Then I quickly push it through the letter hole and walk away. There! I shove my hands in my pockets and bury my chin in my scarf.

Dr. Love, out for a midnight stroll.

I take a deep breath and the frosty air tickles the back

of my throat. I wish there was a channel straight from my mouth to my brain so that the wind could get in there and blow away all the extra thoughts I seem to be having lately. My brain feels like my bedroom. A lot of things are on shelves or in boxes or cupboards or hanging up in the closet or in the drawers under my bed. I know where to find them. But there is this other stuff—comics, football cards, dirty laundry, schoolwork, the busted horn from my bike—lying around, so thick I feel as if it's going to trip me up. I don't even recognize some of it. I feel the same way about my brain. Who's been piling things up in there? Heck, I don't need the wind—I need a shovel!

Will my sister marry Mr. Odsburg? It seems impossible, and yet . . .

Could Dr. Arnold fall in love with Miss Garr?

Does *Mein Liebchen* really mean My darling?

I end up turning onto Quigley Street. I'm not sure why. I hardly know why I do anything these days. I hope I don't have some tragic mental disease.

As I make my way through the puddles of streetlight toward the dead end, I'm not sure what I'm hoping for. Maybe I'll get to number twenty-nine and Natasha will be standing at the front door looking out at the night just like before. This time I won't hide. I'll walk right up to her.

"Who are you?" she'll ask.

"People call me Rex Zero."

Then I'll hand her the little black book.

She'll gasp. "I've been looking everywhere for this," she'll say. "Thank you so much, Rex Zero. Here's a dollar."

I shake this thought from my head like a wet dog shaking off water. I don't want money! And she wouldn't say she's been looking everywhere for the book because it isn't hers. Whoever the book belongs to wrote her name down wrong—Nate instead of Natasha.

As I get nearer to twenty-nine, I notice a truck parked out front. It's a big truck with a chrome bulldog on the top of the grille. The engine is rumbling. The headlights are on. The light dazzles my eyes, but squinting through it, I can see a brown suitcase sitting on the edge of the front porch.

She's leaving!

But no. The front door opens and a man steps out onto the porch, still putting on his coat. Then right behind him steps Natasha Lavender. I stop behind a telephone pole. She's not in white tonight. She's in black. Black high heels, black tight skirt, and a black turtleneck sweater. Her blond hair is piled up on top of her head, held in place by a black comb.

I pick my way through the shadows to the driveway of twenty-seven Quigley, which runs right beside number twenty-nine. There's a hedge separating the two properties and from behind it I can see them standing in profile under the porch light. He's an inch shorter than her, but stocky, strong. He's searching through the pockets of his plaid winter jacket for something. His lighter. He pulls out his cigarettes and lights up. He's not looking at her. He's looking out at the truck.

"Drive safe," she says.

"Why, how thoughtful of you," he says. I recognize his voice. It's Mr. Nasty, all right. "I'll phone," he says. "Soon as I get to Petawawa. And when I hit North Bay, too. And then Sudbury and the Soo. And you'd better be in, you hear?"

She looks tired. "Larry, we've been through this . . ."

"Yeah, yeah, yeah." He takes a drag on his cigarette and picks up his suitcase. He's still not looking at her, still not moving.

"Watch your step, Tasha," he says. "You hear what I'm saying?"

"Yes, Larry. The whole street can hear you."

"That's enough of your lip!" He says. Then he chuckles. "You got enough trouble with your lip without you should be exercising it all the time."

I can't believe he said that.

She opens her mouth to say something but changes her mind. She wraps her arms around herself and bows her head. Larry's fist tightens on the suitcase.

"It's going to get better," she says.

"What? Your face?"

"Larry, please . . ."

"Oh, right!" he crows. "Now I know what you mean. I'm back in the saddle. Got a job. Yippee-aie-oh-ky-aye! A two-week stint hauling hand warmers to Winnipeg. Hand warmers, for the love of Pete!"

"It's a start. And I don't mind us living on my salary . . ."

She covers her mouth. It was the wrong thing to say. He turns very slowly to look at her.

"Thanks for reminding me," he says. Then he starts down the steps, shaking his head the whole way and muttering to himself.

"Aren't you going to kiss me goodbye?" she says.

He stops at the bottom of the stairs and finally he turns to look up at her. He takes another long drag on his cigarette, then blows out the smoke. "Why bother," he says. "It's like you forgot how."

"Larry, I'm sorry . . ."

"Ah, can it, Tash. 'I'm sorry, I'm sorry, I'm sorry.' You should hear yourself." He jumps up on the running board, opens the passenger-side door, and shoves his suitcase into the cab of the truck. He shuts the door, takes one last drag on his cigarette and flicks it away, then jumps back down to the street.

"You do some thinking while I'm gone."

She nods.

He seems to have something stuck on his lip, a piece of tobacco maybe. He worries at it with his tongue and then spits.

"Good," he says. But the way he says it isn't good. He walks around the front of the truck. I press myself into the hedge. If he looks this way he'll see me, but he's got other things on his mind.

"Take care," she says.

He doesn't answer, just climbs up into the cab of his truck and closes the door behind him. Then he puts the truck in gear and pulls away from the curb. I watch it rumble down the street, stop, and turn left onto Fifth.

By the time I round the bushes to her pathway, Natasha is already closing the front door. I pause for just one second on the bottom step and then scramble up.

She turns and looks out at me, curious. She knows everyone in the building, I guess, and I'm not one of them. My heart is beating hard as I step up to the door. Then I go cold all over.

Her eye.

Her right eye is black-and-blue. She lifts her hand to her cheek. She opens the door to her apartment, then turns to see if I'm still there. I open the front door.

"What is it?" she says.

"Natasha?"

"Yes? Who are you?"

I don't answer. I pull the little black book from my pocket and hand it to her. She looks confused. Then she opens it.

"What is this?"

"I found it."

Her forehead creases. She flips through the pages. Then

her eyes light up. She's in the L section. She closes the book. Holds it to her chest. She looks at me again.

"Your eye," I say.

"It's nothing," she says. "Walked into something . . . the corner of a cupboard. Where did you get this?"

"I found it. I'm sorry. I phoned, but . . ."

"A week ago," she says. I nod. I rub my hands on my pant legs. Her face clouds over. "And today?" she says. "Did you call today?"

I don't exactly nod but she knows I did. The muscles in her face tense up. There is rage in her eyes. I step backward, afraid that she's going to slug me or yell or something, although I can't believe she would. Then her expression changes and she looks . . . I'm not sure what . . . doomed?

"I'm really sorry."

She rolls her upper lip inside her mouth. She squeezes her eyes shut. It looks as if she's going to cry, but to my surprise she laughs, and then covers her mouth with her hand.

"I phoned today because I wanted to tell you about the address book," I say. "Then when a man answered, I got all confused."

"I know the feeling."

"He got really steamed."

She nodded. "He does that."

"I'm sorry, Miss Lavender."

"Mrs. Lavender," she corrects me. Then she looks away

and laughs, again, but not because anything is funny. "Mrs. Lavender," she says again.

She wipes her eye, the one that isn't black-and-blue. Then she looks at me. I guess I'm shaking, because she suddenly looks worried. "You'd better step inside," she says.

I do and she reaches around me to close the front door.

"What's your name?"

"Rex. Rex Zero."

Her brow puckers, then she sighs. She's thinking—I don't know what—and I hold my breath so I won't disturb her. I could probably hold my breath for twenty minutes right now! She is just as beautiful in black as she was in white.

She taps the book gently against her leg. Then, as if she has suddenly remembered that I am there, she smiles at me. It's a wobbly smile—a smile with training wheels. She holds up the book. "I'll make sure this gets back to its owner," she says.

I breathe again. "Thanks."

She opens the door to 2B and waves goodbye. "Well, thanks, Rex."

"Watch where you walk," I say.

A MAN'S GOT TO DO

When I get home things seem to have settled down. I stand in the vestibule listening to the warmth. There is still the smell of roast meat in the air. The dishwasher is on in the kitchen, the heat clangs in the radiators. I can hear the television in the TV room upstairs, the faint sound of a radio from behind the door of one of my sisters' rooms.

I'm just about to go up when I go cold all over. The rough draft of my letter to Miss Garr! I don't remember what I did with it.

Without knocking I open the door to my father's study. He's standing on a footstool reaching up to replace a book on the highest shelf. He turns awkwardly and sees me. He looks red in the face. He's a big man, a bit overweight, and it's a long way up.

"Oh, sorry," I say.

"That's all right, chum," says Dad. He quickly stuffs the book in among the others. It's a very old-looking book, thick and red with gold decorations on the spine. The whole shelf is stacked with old books. Ancient history, I guess. Dad loves history.

He dusts off his hands and steps down off the footstool. "What can I do for you?"

I cross the room, glancing at the desktop. The Dr. Love letter isn't there. Either he's got it or I took it to my room. Now that I'm here I'm pretty sure I took it to my room. I figure I'll find out soon enough.

"Looking for something?"

"Uh, some homework."

"Ah, yes. The redoubtable Miss Fish. How is that going?"

Strange he should mention my teacher. I can't tell from his face if he saw the letter or not. But he doesn't look like he's going to give me a talking-to. He just looks a little flustered.

"She's pretty terrible," I say. "But maybe things will get better."

"Well, let's hope," he says.

"I was typing," I say. "Something for school."

I glance at him nervously.

"Well, I didn't find anything," he says.

I turn to go and then I remember something else. Life has gotten so complicated, I forgot all about my list of mysteries to solve.

"What is it, son?"

"Mum says you have something to tell me."

His brow puckers. "Hmmm," he says. "Really? What kind of something?"

I shrug.

"I think I already mentioned the robotic gyropter I'm building in the garage?"

"Dad."

"Was it my upcoming trip to Brazil to capture the wild meringue-utang?"

"What?"

"It's a distant cousin of the orangutan, only tastier."

I roll my eyes. "Something real, Dad."

"Ah, well, why didn't you say?"

"Something about the war, maybe?"

The fun drains from his face. "What makes you think that?"

I try to remember exactly what Mum said that evening they went out on their date. She was fishing for something. I told her the cheese and sniper story but that wasn't what she was after.

Suddenly, I feel uncomfortable, as if Mum was snooping, and I shouldn't have brought it up.

"Well, it was right after Remem . . . I mean Armistice Day. I guess that's why I figured it was about . . . you know . . ."

Dad sits in the easy chair. He picks up his pipe. Then he picks up the little gizmo he uses to clean it out.

"I think I know what you're talking about," he says. He

doesn't look up. I walk closer to him. "There are things Mum thinks you need to know, being the oldest male in the family."

"You mean stuff the girls don't know about?"

He nods. "It's not for delicate ears."

I can't believe it! Something my older sisters don't know. They always act as if they know everything.

"But I'm not sure that now's the time."

"It's not that late," I say.

"No, I don't mean that. I mean now as in you're only eleven. There will be plenty of time to tell you things. In fact, I plan on telling you something useful every day for the next few years. By sixteen you'll know everything there is to know—you won't even have to go to university."

I pull up the footstool he had been standing on and sit down right beside his knee. "So, let's start," I say.

He glares at me under his bushy eyebrows, but it's only his fake glare. "All right," he says. "Here's something useful. When you are in India, check your boots every morning for scorpions."

"Seriously, Dad. You know what I mean."

He stalls some more as if cleaning his pipe has suddenly become a really complicated task. "Maybe she was referring to the time I ordered a boat for the squadron from Supply and Services and they misread my request and sent us a gravy boat. My God, that was something. The whole squadron crossing the Rhine in a gravy boat."

I jump up, pushing back the footstool so hard it tips over.

"Stop it!" I shout. It startles him. Startles me!

"Excuse me, young man?"

"I'm not a kid, Daddy."

"You are, you know."

"Yeah, but I'm not a baby."

He stares at me. His keen hazel eyes are full of me. I can see me there—two of me. And *my* eyes are full of my father: gray hair at the temples, gray wiry hairs poking out of his shaggy eyebrows, nut brown skin. He always looks as if he has a tan even in the middle of winter.

His face seems pained for a moment and then the pain seems to pass. Is he sick? Is that the secret he won't tell me?

"No, you're not a baby, Rex," he says at last. "Despite this little tantrum. Thank you for reminding me. You are growing like a beanstalk. A scarlet runner." He pauses to get his pipe going and the next time he looks my way it is through a cloud of sweet peach-smelling smoke. "I will endeavor not to treat you like a child in the future, and I apologize if I seem to be avoiding your question."

The smoke clears a bit and we lock eyes again.

Suddenly, I want to sit on his knee like I used to, which is ridiculous because I just told him I'm not a baby anymore. I guess it's the look on his face that makes me feel that way, as if he'd prefer that I *were* a baby.

"There are things . . ." He pauses. "Life presents you

with certain . . . challenges." He pauses again. And it's weird because my father is never at a loss for words. He looks up and smiles faintly. "It's just like the cowboys say: 'A man's got to do what a man's got to do.'" His cowboy accent is pretty bad. I don't think there are many cowboys in Wales.

"Your mother is right," he says. "There are things I probably need to let go of. And I will. I will." He swings his hand in the air, kind of grandly, as if an audience has suddenly materialized out of the smoke. "I will tell you when you're ready. And . . . when I'm ready." He looks uncomfortable again.

Suddenly, I wonder if what Mum wanted him to tell me was really about the war, after all. Maybe she was fishing to see if he'd explained to me about the birds and the bees. I pick up the footstool and place it back against the wall.

I've often wondered what birds and bees have to do with sex. When Burt Lancaster kissed Deborah Kerr on the beach in *From Here to Eternity*, I didn't see any bees. And when I see pictures of Marilyn Monroe, I'm sure those aren't birds she's got in her sweater!

I sort of know this stuff, but I don't think I really want to hear about it right now. Not from Dad! It's like when Buster wanted us to see his brother's magazine. I would have looked if James wanted to, but I was glad he didn't. Glad there was a mystery to solve instead.

"Rex, is there anything the matter?"

All of a sudden there's a *lot* the matter! "No, Dad," I say.

"It's okay. I'll be fine." That was exactly what Natasha said, and now *I* feel uncomfortable.

"Are you sure?"

"Yes," I snap. Then I say it again, more politely. "Yes, sir."

"Good," he says. He sounds relieved. "Now, if you're not too old for it, how about a kiss goodnight?"

I kiss his stubbly cheek. Mr. Nasty had stubbly cheeks, too. And as I leave the study I find myself thinking about Natasha kissing him.

Aren't you going to kiss me goodbye?

I wish I hadn't thought about that. I have to pull myself up the stairs holding the railing tightly. My legs are wobbly and I don't know why. Not exactly, anyway.

OH, REX. IT'S YOU!

I t is a moonless night. An icy wind howls down Quigley Street. She is sitting by the window in her upstairs apartment. She is in white again, but her clothes are in tatters and there are deep scratches on her arm, her cheek. Her desperate eyes scan the street. She clears the fog away from the glass with ghostly pale fingers.

There is a growl behind her. She flinches but doesn't look back. Still, she sees him in the reflection on the window striding back and forth, his head low between his shoulders like a lion. Back and forth—a lion in a cage. Every now and then he strikes out. A lamp crashes to the floor. A radio smashes against the wall.

Oh, Rex. Where are you?

"What did you say?"

"Nothing," she squeals. "Nothing, Larry."

"Just like you," he says. "Nothing."

She starts to cry.

"Stop your sniveling!" he shouts. He strides toward her, his hand raised. "Why I oughta . . ."

She cowers against the window, her arms raised across her face.

"No, Larry. Not again, please, I beg of you."

He looms over her and growls. A hideous smile transforms his features into the face of a monster. "Let's see you beg," he murmurs. He forms his hand into a fist and she screams.

Behind them the door crashes open. A masked boy stands there, his own fists of steel at the ready. He steps over the rubble of the shattered door with the brass numbers that read 2B dangling now by a single nail.

"Step away from her, Lavender, if you know what's good for you."

Larry's face contorts with fear. "The masked boy," he says. He whimpers and backs off toward the farthest corner, knocking over furniture as he makes his retreat. Falling, crawling on his hands and knees.

"Are you all right, ma'am?"

"I am now!" she cries, and races from the window to the masked boy at the door. She falls to her knees and throws her arms around his waist. He pats her blond head gently but never takes his eyes off the animal snarling in the corner.

"Looks like I got here just in time," says the masked boy.

She nods and presses her body against his leg. Then,

reaching up with trembling hands, she removes the mask from his face.

"Oh, Rex. It's you!"

◎ ◎ ◎

I wake up with my bedclothes all in a snarl. It's as if a giant boa constrictor has got me and I have to wrestle my way to freedom. At last I'm free. Out of breath, but free. The bedclothes are in a pile on the floor. The cool settles down around me and for now it feels good because I'm burning up.

I take a deep breath, trying to calm my racing heart. I stare into the dark and see her face. Natasha. There are no claw marks, just that awful bruise on her cheekbone near her eye.

She didn't get that from walking into something. He did it. Larry. And I know why. I remember his voice on the telephone.

You think I don't know?

I swallow hard. I thought it was me he was threatening—me he was going to beat up. I was wrong. There is someone else. But it's still my fault she got hit.

What have I done?

THE WATCHER

I head over to Quigley Street after school the next day. I need to apologize properly for what I did. I want to make it up to Natasha Lavender somehow. I want to do something—anything. Make her laugh. Make Larry disappear.

I imagine I'm Rex Zero, King of Everything.

"Mr. Lavender, WE have decided that you must move to Vancouver. Either Vancouver or the North Pole. You have a choice."

"What if I don't wanna move, Your Majesty?"

"Then WE will have to put you in a dungeon with rats. Forever."

Kings always say WE when they mean I. It must make them feel big.

Then I imagine I'm a world-famous surgeon.

"Mrs. Lavender, I can fix that cleft lip of yours so that it will be as perfect as the rest of your lovely face."

"Oh, thank you, Dr. Zero."

But the thing is, I don't want to fix her cleft lip because it doesn't need fixing. I want to tell her that what Larry said about her was stupid. She already is beautiful—and she is crazy to listen to someone like that.

But I don't see her that day.

The next day James comes with me just for something to do. I haven't told the others about what happened, but I tell James. I know he won't laugh. He doesn't. He doesn't say anything for a long time.

Then he says, "Whoa, Rex!"

"What?"

"The wrong name in the phone book. I just figured it out."

I wait and watch his eyes. I can almost see the wheels turning in his head. They're quiet, though. He keeps them well oiled.

"She told you she would return the book to its owner, right?"

"Yes."

"So, obviously she knows him." He looks at me to see if I get it. "She's got a boyfriend."

"I already thought of that," I say. "But you'd think her boyfriend would know how to spell her name."

"Aha!" says James, just the way Perry Mason does when he cracks a case. "Think, Rex."

"I'm all thinked out."

"The man who owned that address book doesn't want *someone* to know he knows a woman named Natasha Lavender. Why?"

I stop in the middle of the sidewalk. "In case someone else looks through the address book?"

James nods.

Then I slap my forehead. Of course! "Natasha's boyfriend is married, too?"

"Bingo!"

I feel great for about one second. Then I think how sad it is. Natasha has found a boyfriend—maybe even a nice one for a change—but he's already married. They both are. They are both trapped forever.

Suddenly I feel kind of weird walking up and down Quigley Street. I'm afraid the neighbors are going to get suspicious and call the cops. So we leave.

But Friday, I get the best excuse ever to go back. Miss Garr hands out the raffle tickets three days early.

Every student is supposed to sell twenty raffle tickets at twenty-five cents a shot, for a basket of fruit courtesy of Thomas Garr's Fine Fruit Market. I know I'll be able to sell at least two tickets to Mum and Dad, and maybe a third to Mr. Odsburg. Vegetarians eat lots of fruit, I bet. I'll also be able to sell one to my next-door neighbor. Not the one whose cat got shot by Annie. Anyway, that will leave sixteen raffle tickets. And I'm going to sell all of them on Quigley Street! It's the perfect cover.

So Friday, I'm over there like a shot, right after school, but before I've gotten up the nerve to even knock on one single door, I see something that makes me forget all about the raffle.

Larry Lavender.

The truck isn't there. But I spot him hanging around in the alley off Quigley Street.

The alley is narrow and full of potholes, with garbage all over the place. On one side, there is a tall wooden fence covered in graffiti. Through missing and busted slats you can see an abandoned factory yard littered with broken-down machinery and oil drums. Larry's standing behind the fence. I stare at him but he doesn't pay any attention to me.

What happened to Winnipeg? It's been less than a week since he left. What's he up to?

I hide behind a garbage can and watch. It doesn't take me long to figure it out. He's spying—spying on his own house!

Watch your step, Tasha. You hear what I'm saying?

"It's a trap," says Buster.

"I bet he never even left town," says James.

It's Friday evening and we're sleeping over at Buster's place. Sami is there, too. Kathy couldn't come. No girls allowed.

"We've got to do something," I say. "What if her friend comes over?"

"He'll kill them both," says Sami.

"The boyfriend?" says Buster.

"No, *Larry*," says Sami. "Probably with a meat cleaver."

"And then wrap them up in canvas and drop them in the Ottawa, way downriver."

"No one will ever find them."

"There will just be the letter on the kitchen table," I say.

"What letter?" says Buster.

"The letter that *looks* like Natasha's handwriting."

"Yeah, it will read: 'I can't live with you another day, Larry. I've run off with Tyrone, who really loves me. Goodbye forever. May you rot in hell! Yours truly, Natasha.' "

"So Larry's off the hook?"

"Except for the detective," I say, "who finds one of her bloodstained high heels in the back of Larry's truck under a pile of hand warmers."

Everybody stares at me.

"What are hand warmers?" says Buster.

"I don't know. Something Larry was supposed to be delivering to Winnipeg."

"Wow!" says Sami.

"You should be a writer," says James.

"Or a murderer," says Buster.

Later, Buster sneaks one of his brother's girlie magazines and we all take a look. Sami laughs so much we're afraid that Buster's mother will come, so we put a pillow over his head. James gets really quiet as Buster turns the pages. Buster is breathing funny.

"Have you got a cold?" I ask him. The thing is, I feel sort of strange, too. When I see one of my sisters in her underwear, it's no big deal. But this is different.

In Buster's brother's magazine there is a woman with hair the exact same color as Natasha's. I start thinking of Natasha in black underwear and then I *really* feel strange. I look at James, who is looking at his watch. "Isn't it time for *Shock Theatre*?" he says.

It is, and we all troop down to the rec room to watch Gorgo destroy London. A good monster movie is a sure bet to help take your mind off women in black underwear.

We talk and laugh late into the night, then one by one everyone falls asleep, but not me. I lie there thinking about a lot of things and trying *not* to think about a lot of things. One of the things I do think about is Kathy. How great it would be if she were here, because she's just one of the guys, after all. But then I realize that, really, she isn't. And she never will be.

In the school yard at lunchtime today when Buster invited us over, she looked kind of glum.

"Sorry, Kathy," Buster said. "It's boys only."

"Who cares," Kathy said, but it looked like she cared. "And anyway, I couldn't come even if I wanted to. Dr. Arnold is taking us out for dinner."

"You, too?"

"All of us. Mom, Missy, and me. We're going to the Lucky Key."

That got a groan from Buster. "Yuck. Chinese."

Buster doesn't like any food he hasn't already had before. It's amazing he didn't starve to death when he was a baby.

Later, I saw Kathy standing alone by the fence and I went to talk to her.

"Too bad about tonight," I said.

She shrugged. "Honest, I don't care."

"So, what's eating you?"

She shrugged again. Her fingers were woven through the links in the fence. She leaned against it. Then she leaned back until her arms were fully extended. Her knuckles turned white.

She gave me this worried look. "Did you send the letter?"

"Sure," I said. "On Tuesday."

"Oh." She pulled herself back toward the fence, pressing her cheek against it.

"I thought you wanted me to."

She looked at me and sighed. "I did," she said. "But maybe it wasn't such a good idea."

"Now you tell me!"

"Sorry," she said. "I know. It's just that . . ."

"It's just that what?"

"Dr. Arnold is . . . well, it turns out he's kind of nice."

I hadn't been thinking about the letter since I sent it.

Now I thought of it actually arriving at Miss Garr's place. Miss Garr actually opening it and reading it.

"He doesn't try too hard, you know, to make me like him or anything," said Kathy. "He's funny, too. He makes me laugh."

I couldn't believe she said that, but it got worse.

"My mom is so happy," she said.

Yikes!

INCIDENT AT THE TWO-BY-FOUR

I don't get home from Buster's on Saturday until almost noon. Everybody is out except Mum and Annie Oakley. Annie's not feeling well. She's in bed and Mum is doing laundry.

"I'm heading out," I yell down the laundry chute.

"Eat something," Mum yells back.

I make a peanut butter sandwich and hightail it. I lick the peanut butter off my fingers, stick my hands in my parka pockets, and head toward Bank Street.

Dark clouds hang over the city like big bags of dirty laundry. Snow clouds? I hope.

I head toward you know where, but I'm beginning to wonder if maybe Natasha went on a trip. Maybe she left for good—ran off with her boyfriend! But if she did, Larry would have noticed since he's spying on her.

Where is he staying? Where did he leave the truck? I'm just passing the corner of Fourth, kind of lost in thought, when I look up and there she is on the other side of the street, turning onto Bank Street from Fifth. I stop and a Saturday shopper bumps into me.

"Sorry," I say, stepping aside. Then when I look again, Natasha is gone. I race across Bank Street and a car beeps at me.

"Sorry!" I shout.

I hurry along the sidewalk. Where did she go? Luckily, I catch a glimpse of her out of the corner of my eye. She has just stepped into the café on the corner of Bank and Fifth. It's so small they call it the Two-by-Four. I peer through the glass. There is a man at a table rising to greet her. He gently takes her arm and kisses her on the cheek.

It's not Larry, that's for sure.

I step back from the glass before she notices me. Then an idea pops into my head and I dart to the corner and look east down Fifth.

Just as I suspected—her husband! He must have been tailing her and he's not even half a block away. I pull my head back and lean against the wall.

What do I do?

There's only one thing I can do. I dash into the café and go straight to their table. Natasha is sitting down now, pulling off her gloves.

"Rex? What are you doing here?"

I lean on the table, out of breath. "He's coming!" I whisper.

"Excuse me?"

"You know," I whisper, glancing furtively at her friend. He's smiling, but his smile wavers when he sees the expression on my face.

"I don't understand," says Natasha.

"Larry! He didn't go away."

She clutches the edge of the table.

"He's almost here!"

I'm trying to keep it down but people are turning to look anyway.

Her friend jumps up. "I'll wait in the men's room," he says.

As soon as he goes, I sit down in his seat.

"What are you doing?" says Natasha.

"You can pretend I'm an orphan and you're buying me a cup of hot chocolate. That'll be your cover."

She almost smiles. "Scoot!" she says.

I jump to my feet and head toward the men's room.

"Rex!"

I turn. She's pointing, panic-stricken, at the seat opposite her. Her friend left his coat. I grab it, almost knocking over the chair, and scurry toward the back of the café.

As I reach the door to the men's room, I glance back. A waitress is talking to Natasha. And Larry walks by the front window, his collar up, glancing inside. For a split second, he stops, sees her, then moves on.

That was close!

I hand the coat to Natasha's friend. "Thank you," he says. "Thank you."

I nod. Now what do we do? He doesn't seem to know. I peek through the door. Natasha has produced a thick paperback from her handbag and is reading it. There is no Larry at the window.

The friend peeks over my shoulder. "Where did he go?"

"He walked by," I say. "But he saw her, all right."

The man steps back into the men's room and leans against the wall. He wipes his face slowly with his hand. "Oh my," he says. "Oh my, my, my."

He's what my dad would call a nice-looking bloke. He's got wavy ginger-colored hair and blue eyes. He's no Cary Grant. He's kind of ordinary-looking and a little scrawny, but he's got an open face. And that open face of his looks pretty worried.

I close the door. "He's been spying on her," I say. "He didn't go away."

Mr. Boyfriend's jaw drops. "You must be kidding?"

"No, sir."

He sighs and shakes his head. Then he wipes his face again with his hand.

I peek through the door. The waitress has brought Natasha a pot of tea.

"I could go scout things out," I say.

Mr. Boyfriend frowns.

"He doesn't know me," I say. "It'll be safe."

Now he closes his eyes and his head droops. When he looks at me again he's smiling in a worried kind of way.

"This is pathetic," he says. "Here I am hiding in a bathroom completely dependent upon a very brave young man of . . . what? Eleven?"

"Bingo!"

He holds out his hand. "Wilfred Dance," he says. "And I have a feeling you're the young man I should be thanking for the return of my address book."

I shake his hand. "That's me," I say. "Rex Zero."

He takes a long, deep breath and opens the door a smidgen. "What do you suppose we do, Mr. Zero?"

"Well, I could go check out the street. Let you know what's up."

Mr. Dance combs his fingers through his hair. He walks to the sink and looks in the mirror.

"I'm not cut out for this kind of thing," he says. "I'm a librarian, not James Bond."

It's true he's no secret agent man. So I guess it will have to be me making all the decisions around here.

Just then the door opens and Mr. Dance and I both gasp. The man looks from one to the other of us, makes a crabby face, and hurries into the cubicle.

"Does Larry know what you look like?" I ask in a whisper.

"I don't think so."

"You didn't . . . you haven't been over . . ."

"Over to Natasha's? No," he says. "Never. Certainly not."

I peek through the door again. This time Natasha looks at me with an anxious expression. I close the door quickly. The toilet flushes. The crabby guy will be out any second and the men's room isn't big enough for the three of us.

"Come on," I say, grabbing Mr. Dance by the sleeve. "You can pretend to be my uncle. We'll leave here together."

"What about Natasha?"

I hold open the door and he steps out, but we stand there uncertainly in the narrow hallway leading to the kitchen until the waitress comes by, her hands full of plates of hot chicken sandwiches.

"Are we having a party?" she says in a tetchy voice.

I head to the front door and glance back at Mr. Dance. "I'll make sure he's not around. You can talk to Natasha until I give you the high sign. Okay?"

"Whatever you say."

Natasha smiles at me as I go by and my heart starts to flutter, but I don't have time to dillydally. I've got a job to do. I step outside into the cold.

It's starting to snow.

The sidewalk is busy. Shoppers hurry by with shopping bags and bundle buggies, holding on to their hats, foreheads creased against the cold.

Larry is nowhere in sight. I lean against the window, my

arms crossed, looking both ways, acting nonchalant. When I peer back into the café, Mr. Dance is leaning on the table talking to Natasha. She says something back to him in an urgent way.

I wish I could read lips. All spies have to learn that. Then I remember my job and look up and down Bank.

There he is! North of us, about three shops up, hanging out in the entranceway. I quickly look the other way. I count five steamboats. Then I casually enter the café.

"He's just up the street," I say.

"Oh God," says Mr. Dance.

"You'd better go," says Natasha. "We'll talk later."

He nods. Then he takes her hand and squeezes it. I turn away because it's kind of personal. But it's also exciting, like a war movie. The brave soldier and the nurse, and—out there on the street—the jealous Gestapo officer, a Luger in his hand.

Mr. Dance and I walk up Bank right past Larry, who doesn't even glance at us as we go by. His eye is trained on the Two-by-Four.

"Was that him?"

"Yeah, it was."

I hope he's going to say something, but he seems lost in thought. I wonder if he would take me somewhere for a hot chocolate. It's getting really cold and the snow is coming down heavy now.

Finally, we stop. He's got the goodbye look in his eyes. He shakes my hand again. "Thanks, Rex, for saving my bacon."

I like that. It's just the kind of thing Humphrey Bogart would say.

ERIK AT NINE

By the next day, the world is a winter wonderland. There are mounds of snow on the lawns up and down Clemow Avenue. Enough snow to build one of those snowmen you see on Christmas cards with a carrot nose and two eyes made out of coal. Enough snow to build an igloo for a family of eight. Enough snow to take your sled out to Hog's Back Park.

But in the Norton-Norton household, no one is going sledding or igloo-building or snowman-making. No one is going anywhere, except maybe for a nice drive in the country. It's Sunday again.

Armistice Day didn't change anything. Like those prisoners who break out of jail only to be tracked down by bloodhounds, I made my escape, but I'm back in the pen. When I'm grown up, my kids will *have* to play on Sundays. It will be a rule.

Mum wants to cross the river to Quebec and drive up

into the Gatineau Hills to look at the mountains. They're not really mountains—not like in Vancouver. They're more like bumps.

"But," says Dad, "they're the oldest bumps in the world. That's why they're so low. It's hard work standing around looking majestic all day."

I peer into Annie's room. She's too sick to go for the family drive. Lucky her. Cassie isn't going either. She and Mr. Odsburg are going skating. There seem to be only two ways to avoid going out on a Sunday drive in the Pontiac with your entire family: get sick or go steady. I guess I'd rather get sick.

I step into Annie's room. It should be good and full of germs. I take a deep breath. She stirs and raises her head from the pillow just enough to see that I'm there.

"Hi," she says. It's almost the nicest thing she's ever said to me.

"I was just seeing if I could get sick by coming in your room."

"Be my guest," she says.

Boy, she must be really sick. I sit on the edge of her bed. She doesn't look my way. She's pale and her eyes are hooded, as if holding them open is difficult.

"I didn't find the hidden cache," she says.

I don't know what she's talking about. I wonder if she's got malaria and is going demented.

"What do you mean?"

"Daddy," she says.

"No, it's Rex."

She lifts her head a little and tries to give me one of her death stares. Then her head falls back on the pillow.

"I meant *Daddy's* secret cache," she says. "Where he's hiding the you know what."

The letter. Now I remember. The letter written in German.

"I looked everywhere," she says.

Her voice is so weak that she doesn't sound as scary as usual.

"Annie," I say, "Dad may have some letter written in German, but he's not a spy or anything."

She doesn't look at me, but she manages a weak growl and slobbers on her pillow.

"Yuck!" she says, moving her head away from the stain. "Look what you made me do."

I hand her the box of Kleenex. She takes a halfhearted swipe at the mess and throws the tissue into a brown paper bag on the floor overflowing with used tissues.

"I know he's not a spy, Rex," she says. "Spies don't get letters that start with 'My Darling.' "

Then Mum comes to the door.

"Isn't this lovely," she says. "How thoughtful of you, Rex."

Annie groans.

And then Mum says, "Why don't you stay here, if you like, and keep your big sister company."

I can hardly believe my ears. I look at Annie, expecting her to shriek, but she doesn't.

"Okay," I say.

Saved. And I didn't even have to get sick! I call goodbye from the top of the stairs. Flora Bella is angry because she has to go. Mum has to drag her through the front door. Eventually, it slams shut and a few moments later the car is backing down the driveway.

I head back to Annie's room and find her sitting up, her hands crossed in her lap.

"That was quick," I say.

"I was faking it."

She still looks sick. I've never seen her so white. But she's not as sick as she was pretending to be. There is even a twinkle in her eye.

"I didn't find Dad's cache, but I did find something," she says. She reaches under her pillow and brings out a photograph.

There is a woman and a boy in the picture, leaning against the front of a car. The boy is about Flora Bella's age. The woman has her arm around his shoulder—mother and son, by the looks of it. The photo is black-and-white, but you can tell she's brunette and he's blond. She is wearing her hair in plaits. That's what Mum calls them when she does

Flora Bella's hair. I think real people call them braids. The woman is thin and pretty. The boy's hair is curly. He has his hand up to shield his eyes from the sun. He's smiling, but in a serious way. He's wearing those leather shorts with suspenders that German people wear, a white shirt, open at the neck, and sandals with straps.

I stare at the picture. Then I turn it over. On the back is written "Erik at nine."

"Where did you find this?"

"It was under the big chair. Must have fallen there."

I study the photo. I don't know what to think.

"He looks like you," says Annie.

"What do you mean?"

"Just look."

"So he's got blond hair," I say. "Lots of people have blond hair."

She grabs the picture and stares at it. Holding it with both hands, she slowly sinks back onto her pillow. Her cheeks are red from the effort of sitting up, and her forehead is sweaty. She looks mesmerized, but I'm not sure if it's the picture or her fever.

"I feel like I know him," she says.

Suddenly, I wish I *had* gone for a drive in the country. I hate it in here. It's stuffy and germy. I stand up, shove my hands in my pockets, and walk to her window to look out at the snow. I want to bury myself in it.

"It's strange," she says. "Don't you feel it—like you know him?"

"No!" I shout. "It's just some boy." I rest my forehead against the cool glass. My pulse is racing. I'm burning up. Maybe I've got what she's got.

"Do you know what I think?" she says.

I stamp my foot. "I don't care what you think, okay? So just shut up!"

She raises herself on one elbow. "We've got to find that cache, Rex."

"Why?"

"So we can know for sure."

"Know what?"

She looks as if she's sorry for me.

"Stop it!" I shout. I'm boiling mad now.

I know what she's getting at. I'm not a baby. A letter that says "My Darling" written in German. A hidden photograph of a pretty woman from some time ago, by the look of it, with a nine-year-old son. Does she think I'm stupid?

"You're wrong!" I shout at her.

"About what?"

"Whatever you're thinking." And I'm just about to shout some other things when she shushes me up so forcefully I almost choke on my own words.

In the silence I hear the front door open and then Mum's voice sings out.

"Hoo-oome," she says.

It can't be. They've only been gone a few minutes.

"Go!" says Annie.

I don't go. I can't move.

"Get out of here!" she says. "Now!"

So I go. At the door, I turn and see her put the photograph back under her pillow. The picture of a complete stranger named Erik, who looks like me. And his mother, who has no name.

THE BOMB

The Sausage is sick. He must have caught what Annie has. They didn't even get out of the city before he had thrown up all over everybody. Flora Bella describes it in detail. I spend the rest of the day in my bedroom trying to read, but the words keep floating around on the page. They won't stay still. Nothing will stay still.

At least, by holing up in my room, I avoid Annie. I don't really believe in the devil, but if there is one, she could get a job with him easy.

◎ ◎ ◎

It's great to leave the house the next day. The snow is still deep and crisp and even, like in that Christmas carol. Christmas! It's less than a month away. The fresh, cold air cleans my head out. No more germs, no more strange boys in leather shorts. Everything is looking brighter by the time I get to school.

And that's when the bomb drops.

Miss Garr stands at the front of the class holding something in her hands. A letter. I recognize the creamy color of the envelope, but it's a lot grimier than it was the day I sent it. Miss Garr is wearing the biggest scowl I have ever seen.

"Someone," she says. "Someone *in this class* has broken the law."

There is a gasp followed by utter silence. Then Susan-Anne-Margaret bursts into tears.

"I'm sorry, Miss Garr," she says. "I'm sorry."

"Susan-Anne-Margaret?"

"My parents bought all my raffle tickets," sobs S-A-M. "I just couldn't go door-to-door. It's too frightening. I'm so, so sorry."

"Oh, for goodness' sake, child, stop that insufferable sniveling." The tone of Miss Garr's voice only makes S-A-M wail all the louder.

"Stop it immediately!"

S-A-M sniffs and sits up, her hands crossed meekly on her desk.

"You silly goose," says Miss Garr. "I'm not talking about raffle tickets. I'm talking about an act of treason. An act of war!" She holds the envelope up for all to see.

"This disgusting piece of filth was mailed to my home address."

Another gasp.

Disgusting?

There was nothing disgusting about the letter, was there? I bite my lip. Did I say something I didn't mean to? I remember how I couldn't concentrate because I was thinking about Natasha. Oh, no. What did I say?

Miss Garr is scanning the class, like a turret gun on a tank. She starts on row one—that's me. I'm blushing so badly I can't bear to look at her, but her gaze travels right on by. Everyone is blushing. Everyone looks guilty.

Finally she makes it to the window aisle and Donnie Dangerfield.

"What is written in this letter is libel," she says, as if she were talking just to him. He doesn't flinch. He stares right back at her. I've never seen him give her so much attention.

"Does anyone know what libel means?" Miss Garr's eyes swivel to Polly. "Miss Goldstein?"

Polly's father is a lawyer and Polly wants to be a lawyer, too. Miss Garr likes to ask her legal questions the way she likes to ask me to sing.

"It means something false?"

"A false and malicious statement, yes. Go on."

But Polly doesn't know or doesn't want to, which hardly matters to Miss Garr because she has her speech already prepared.

"What is written in this letter is a lie. Whoever wrote this vile and repulsive missive intended to hurt the recipient and make a fool of her. The recipient, however, is made of stronger stuff." She pauses to load more ammunition into her vocal cords. "This culprit will be brought to justice."

Again her head swivels around to Donnie. Other people's heads turn to look his way. Donnie just sits there looking relaxed.

How can he act so cool? I ask myself. Then I remember why. He's innocent!

What have I got myself into?

I glance at Kathy. She has turned deathly white right down to her knuckles, which are clenched in fists on her desktop. Me, I'm shaking so much I have to grab hold of the edge of my desk. I'm hot all over. It feels like the flu. I could start puking any second, but I can't ask to leave. She would know. *She would know!*

The room is silent. Not dead silent. It feels more like the room has a giant pulse. A pulse the size of King Kong's. The whole room feels like it might start shaking any second.

"I will give the culprit one day," says Miss Garr, tapping the letter against her open palm. "One day to make himself known to me."

Polly clears her throat. "So, it's a boy, Miss Garr?"

Miss Garr's eyes widen with interest. "What makes you say that, Polly?"

"You said the culprit had a day to make *himself* known to you."

Now Miss Garr glares. "I was merely using correct English, as you know perfectly well, Miss Goldstein. Was that impertinence, young lady?"

Polly looks down at her desk and doesn't answer.

"I asked you a question."

Polly still won't look up.

Then, suddenly breaking the silence, a voice says, "Leave her alone."

It's Zoltan. He's standing.

"Mr. Kádár?"

"She only ask question," he says. "Good question." He looks as if he has more to say, but it will be too hard to say it, so he sits down.

For some reason, this is enough to stop the runaway train. Zoltan is older than us and bigger. His voice is deeper, too, and he looks like someone who has seen even worse teachers than Miss Garr, and he may have eaten one or two of them for lunch. Whatever it is, Miss Garr steps back and takes a deep restorative breath. She stares at the letter in her hand as if it is the source of her power. When she looks up, she smiles a frozen smile.

"I do think it is a boy, since you ask. But I may be wrong. Whoever it is, the person or persons responsible for this gross indecency will identify himself or herself or themselves before nine tomorrow morning or there will be no Christmas party."

The class groans.

"Silence!"

When there is silence, she holds up the envelope by the corners and continues. "You all know Constable Paul?" she says. Constable Paul is the traffic safety cop. "He assures me that the police can lift fingerprints off this envelope." The class stirs excitedly. Miss Garr taps the edge of the envelope like it's not a vile, repulsive missive anymore but an invitation to the ball.

"Constable Paul also assures me he can have a crew of crime-scene investigators come into this room and take every student's prints." A further gasp. "So there will be no escape. We will find the guilty party."

The police taking our fingerprints? It's like a dream come true and everybody starts fidgeting with excitement. Even me, until I remember that it's my prints they're going to find!

Kids turn in their seats to talk to their neighbors. For once Miss Garr lets us. She wants us to be excited. I glance again at Kathy but she won't return my gaze.

Sami leans forward and hums the theme song of *Dragnet* in my ear. *"Dum da dum dum. Dum da dum dum DUM!"*

Everyone wants to know what the letter says. That's what they're all whispering about. I only wish I didn't know.

"I hope Donnie didn't do it," whispers Rhonda. "Garr will kill him this time."

We all look across the room at the class clown. He's

looking out the window at the bright, hard sunshine. I glance toward the front. Miss Garr is staring at him, her eyes glinty with triumph.

Finally, she calls us to order.

"Tomorrow by nine," she says.

She carefully places the envelope on her desk and picks up her notes. "Australia," she says brightly. "Turn to page thirty-eight in your atlas, children."

With trembling fingers I turn to page thirty-eight and stare at that continent sixty billion miles away. If only I were there.

◉ ◉ ◉

"We'll give ourselves up."

James looks at Kathy, Buster, and me. We're in the playground at recess, standing by the fence. James has on his best James Stewart face. Or maybe his Gary Cooper *High Noon* face.

"It's my fault," says Kathy. "If it hadn't been for me, none of this would have happened."

"I wrote it," I say. "I mailed it, too."

"We all approved what you wrote," says James. "We're in this together."

"Not me," says Buster. "I never liked the idea. Anyway, my fingerprints won't be on the letter. I never touched it."

Kathy is ready to punch him, but James stops her. "There was nothing rude or—what did she say—gross? There was nothing gross in the letter."

"It was stupid," mutters Buster. "It was a good joke when we were just talking about it, but I would never have sent it." He won't look at us.

And he's right, in a way. He had hardly anything to do with the letter. But I'm mad at him, all the same. Only, not half so mad as I am with myself. I thought we'd kill two birds with one stone. Looks like we're going to kill four birds with one stone, or three, depending on whether Buster deserts us. The thing is, I never thought the letter would hurt her feelings. Or did I?

"We've got until the start of school, tomorrow," says Kathy.

"Good," says James. "We can sleep on it."

"I'm not going to sleep on it," says Buster.

I don't say it, but I have a feeling I'm not going to sleep at all.

KING OF NOTHING

The jailer shoves me in the cell and slams the door.

"I'm innocent!" I call, rattling the bars. He just walks away, his laughter echoing down the long, dark corridor.

"Well, well, well."

I swing around. There's a man lying on the bottom bunk, his head lost in the shadows until he leans forward. Larry Lavender. He looks me up and down with an evil smirk on his face.

"Look what the cat dragged in," he says. Then he sits up and swings his feet onto the floor.

I lean backward against the cell door.

"I gotta bone to pick with you, kiddo."

I turn to rattle the bars again and gasp. Miss Garr and Constable Paul are standing there.

"That's him, all right, Constable. You work fast."

"Thank you, ma'am," he says, tipping his hat. "This

whippersnapper won't be causing you any more trouble for a long, long time."

They both laugh. Larry laughs, too.

Then, "Rex? Is that you?"

I turn to the right. In the next cell over stands my father, his hands grasping the bars. He hasn't shaved, his clothes are in rags, and he's thin, thin, thin.

"They say I'm a German spy, Rex," he says. "But I'm not a spy. Who did this to me, Rex? Who, who, who?"

"Yeah," says Larry. "Who got us in this mess, eh?" He strides toward me, punching a fist into the palm of his hand.

Miss Garr laughs hysterically. "There will be no Christmas party for the likes of you, Rex Zero."

Constable Paul laughs. Larry laughs. Only my father and I aren't laughing. He's staring at me, shaking his head. "Was it you, Rex? Why?"

"Yes, why?"

There's another cell beyond my father's, and Natasha Lavender is standing there, all in shadows and all in white, a single light shining down on her blond hair, giving her a kind of halo.

"What are you doing here?" I call to her. "You didn't do anything wrong."

She stares at Larry. "He killed Wilfred and I hope he rots in hell for it. But that won't change a thing. I'm alone and will always be alone."

"No!" I cry. "It isn't fair." I rattle the bars as hard as I can.

"It isn't fair. It isn't fair. It isn't fair."

When I wake up, I can still hear a voice somewhere deep inside me crying, "It isn't fair."

It's dark. Winter dark. And cold in my room at the top of the house. I pull my quilted comforter up to my chin, but I can't stop shaking. I've never felt so alone in my whole life.

A REPRIEVE

t's my fault. I'll handle it."

I can't believe I said that! But it sounds good. James and Kathy and I are standing shivering in the school yard Tuesday morning. Buster is nowhere to be seen. I'm a little hurt but not surprised. Kathy grabs my arm and apologizes. I shake her off. I expect James to say something noble, but he seems relieved. I can't really complain. I mean, I offered to take the blame. Except in a movie they would load up their six-guns and say, "We're with you all the way, partner."

Buster is not at school, but he has been blabbing. As soon as I arrive in class, Sami leans forward and whispers in my ear.

"Did you give yourself up?"

"No," I say. "Not yet."

He looks at the clock. So do I. It's almost nine. I try to imagine leaving my desk and heading off to find Miss Garr.

Where does she hang out before class? In a casket in the basement?

But I can't make my feet move. And the clock ticks toward nine.

Finally, Miss Garr comes into the room and the buzz dies immediately. She doesn't even need to call the class to attention. She is back at her turret gun, surveying the battlefield. When she's finished, there is a sly kind of smile on her face for just a moment. But it dies there.

"As you can see," she says, "there is a new development in our unpleasant little mystery."

Everyone looks around. What development?

Donnie Dangerfield is absent! Then the whispers start.

"Enough," she says. "No one has come forward, which suggests that the culprit is too much of a coward to face the consequences of his actions. And *yes*, Polly, I did say 'his.'"

Polly only stares at her desk.

The murmuring starts up again.

"Class, please."

Miss Garr folds her hands in front of her chest as if she's praying. "I will extend the deadline for the confession until tomorrow morning at the same time. Perhaps you can pass that information on to anyone who is not here."

A reprieve. Just like in the movies when the governor calls at the last minute and the falsely accused man is already strapped into the electric chair.

The thing is, nobody is loosening the straps. I'm not free. I have one more day, that's all. Still, I shake with relief so badly I can hardly write the date in the upper-right-hand corner of my notebook.

The relief doesn't last and soon I feel even guiltier. Miss Garr thinks Donnie did it. Other kids in the class probably think so, too.

We work away at our math, but there is too much on my mind to make the numbers do what they're supposed to do. Something is bothering me. That's an understatement! There is lots and lots bothering me. But there is something else—something new—that I can't put my finger on.

And then it comes to me. I'm angry, that's what. Angry that Miss Garr thinks Donnie wrote that letter. Donnie is a great guy, but there is no way he could have written a letter that good.

"Rex, is something the matter?"

I look up and Miss Garr is staring straight at me.

"Question seven," I say.

She sighs. "Sami, help your mathematically inept friend, will you?"

I turn around. Sami smiles and looks at my math notebook. Then he looks up at me and frowns. My page is completely blank.

At recess, Kathy and I tell James what happened.

"A lucky break," he says. "Maybe we can still come up with something."

"What if I tell Dr. Arnold what we did?" says Kathy. "Maybe he would talk to Miss Garr and explain that we did it for my sake."

I can't believe my ears. "Won't he hate you?"

She looks down at the ground. She's building a little canal in the snow with her boot. "He might, but then again he might not." She digs a little deeper. "If I still didn't like him, he might be mad. But what if I tell him how much things have changed?"

"They have?"

She looks up and nods enthusiastically. "We had a really good time when we went out to dinner on Saturday. Missy is really cute and I had a Shirley Temple."

"What's that?"

"A drink served in a glass with a stem and an umbrella and a maraschino cherry—everything except booze." Her happy face droops and she goes back to digging the canal. She breaks through to asphalt.

"Oh, that's just great," I say.

"I'm sorry."

"Yeah, well why couldn't you have liked him two weeks ago?"

She pouts and James frowns at me.

"I'll tell Dr. Arnold," says Kathy. "I'll explain."

"Even if you did tell him, what can he do?" says James. "Miss Garr will be more embarrassed if he talks to her. And she'll still take it out on the class. Right?"

Kathy and I nod. We know it's true.

I try to think of some other way to smooth things out with Miss Garr. Like maybe a steamroller.

◎ ◎ ◎

We're walking up Lyon Street heading home after school when someone calls my name. I turn around.

It's Natasha Lavender.

We wait while she catches up to us. She's wearing a checkered tweed coat, black-and-white, with black boots and gloves, a white scarf, and a woolly white hat.

I introduce her to James and Kathy.

"I wonder if I might have a word with you?" she says.

The others look at me with surprise. I feel strange and a little scared.

"Sure," I say. And then I say goodbye to my friends and they head off up Lyon Street.

"Was that rude of me?" she asks.

"No. It's okay." I glance past her down Lyon Street toward Fifth.

"Larry's not around," she says. "Don't worry about him."

I look into her eyes. "Did you kill him?"

"My God, no!" she says, resting her hand on her chest. Then she laughs. "But it's an idea."

I shake my head. How could I have said that? "I'm sorry, ma'am. It's just that . . ."

"No need to explain," she says. "Shall we walk?" I nod and we head along Lyon toward my place. I'm trying to imagine how I'll introduce her to my mother.

She doesn't speak right away. Then it kind of bursts out of her.

"After I found out from you that Larry had been spying on me, I phoned around. He'd been staying with a pal, borrowed his truck to pull that little charade the other night. He didn't get the job driving to Winnipeg. But as it turned out, he got one driving to Chicago, just yesterday. So he really is gone this time. Until Friday, anyway."

I nod. My head is bursting with questions, but I don't know what to say. Her perfume is making me flustered. Up ahead, James and Kathy are looking back at me. They're a block away, but I can tell they're worried. Part of me wants to run away and be with them. Part of me doesn't.

"Listen," she says. "I owe you for what you did. Are you free for that cup of hot chocolate?" I look at her in case she's kidding. "Are you expected home right away? Would your mother mind?"

Would my mother mind? She's got two sick kids to look after, and, besides, she hardly ever knows where I am.

"Okay," I say, and so we set off down Second toward Bank Street. I wave at Kathy and James. James waves. Kathy just stares.

Natasha and I choose a seat by the front window at the Two-by-Four. I watch her take off her leather gloves, fold them neatly and lay them on the linoleum tabletop. Her black eye is healing, more yellow now than anything. She's covered the worst of the damage with makeup. She takes off her checkered coat and I think about movies where a handsome gentleman leaps to his feet and helps to ease a lady out of her coat. But I just sit there like a lump of Silly Putty.

"There," she says, sitting down across from me. Smiling, she hands me the menu.

I don't order a hot chocolate. I order a bowl of ice cream instead.

"I wanted to explain to you what's going on," she says when the waitress has taken our order.

"You don't have to."

"No, but I don't want you to have the wrong idea." She looks out the window. The sun is low on the horizon. It is rolling down Fifth like a blazing hot bowling ball. She squints and turns back toward me.

"I haven't been sneaking around behind my husband's back. Not really. I don't want you to think I'm that kind of a person."

I nod.

"He—Mr. Dance—is in a very difficult situation. He and

170

his wife are . . . not happy together anymore. One day at work he looked so sad I got talking to him and . . . Well, I guess we both had a lot to talk about. We sometimes meet for tea. That's all, really. Or long walks. Once, when Larry was away, we went to a movie, but I felt so guilty we never did it again."

The waitress brings us our things: coffee for her, Neapolitan ice cream with two ladyfingers for me.

"Listen to me blabbering," she says, when the waitress has gone. "Is this painfully embarrassing for you?"

"No," I say. "Except that . . ." I look down at my ice cream. I have a spoonful of it in my hand, but I don't think I can eat it just yet. There is something I want to say, but I'm afraid to.

"Except what, Rex?"

"Except that Larry hit you."

She picks up her coffee and takes the smallest sip, winces. Too hot.

"He's been out of work for quite a while," she says, placing the cup carefully back on its saucer. "He didn't use to be like that."

I sneak another look at her. She sneaks a look at me and we both smile. This would be a good time to tell her I'm in love with her and we should move to Paris. But I guess she's got enough to deal with.

Still, I wish I could stay here at the Two-by-Four Café forever—far away from Miss Garr or some stupid boy in leather shorts in a stupid photograph or anybody else in the whole world.

I smile again and she smiles again. That is all I want. I want her to smile at me.

She takes a deep breath. "You have been very important to us, Rex," she says. "To Wilfred . . . Mr. Dance and me."

"I have?"

She nods.

"We talked Saturday night on the phone. He likes how brave and resourceful you were. He said it made him want to be brave and resourceful himself."

Brave and resourceful. Ha! If she only knew.

"He phoned again last night to tell me he had finally gotten up the nerve to talk to his wife. To tell her it was over."

"Really? What did she say?"

"She laughed."

"She laughed?"

"She laughed and said, 'It's about time,' and then she left. Just like that."

I lean back in my chair in disbelief. I try to imagine my father and mother talking to each other that way.

And then, suddenly, the picture of the pretty German woman flashes into my mind.

I stare at my ice cream. It's melting—my whole world is melting.

Then Natasha's hand is on mine, squeezing it. Her brow

is creased with worry. "Here I am telling my troubles to an eleven-year-old. I didn't mean to startle you."

She lets go of my hand and picks up her coffee cup.

I take a spoonful of ice cream. I am at the strawberry now. It helps.

When I look up again, she seems on edge. She looks at her watch.

"What are *you* going to do?" I say.

She puts down her cup and stares at it. Then she looks up and her eyes are steely. "When Larry gets home Friday, we're going to have to have a good long talk."

I remember the way Larry likes to talk. "Aren't you afraid—"

"I'm a big girl," she says. "I can look after myself." She seems to want me to agree.

I nod, slowly.

"I'd better be going," she says. She finds her purse, checks the bill, and counts out the change. "You don't need to leave," she says. "Enjoy your ice cream."

"Okay," I say. "Thanks."

I watch her put her coat back on, hurriedly this time, as if Larry might show up at any minute. She pulls on her leather gloves. She looks at me and smiles.

"I really only meant to buy you a treat to thank you for Saturday. I don't know why I got talking like this." She looks cross, all of a sudden, as she does up the big black buttons of her coat. "Don't know what came over me."

"It was nice," I say. "I hope everything works out."

"Me, too," she says. "Thanks again, Rex Zero."

With a little squeeze of my shoulder, she leaves the café. The door jingles behind her. As she passes the window she waves again and manages another little smile.

I finish my ice cream: all the strawberry, then, last of all, the chocolate. I don't want to leave.

I pick up her coffee cup. There's a trace of lipstick on the rim. I close my eyes and bring it to my lips right where the smudge is.

It's our first kiss. Lukewarm and a little bitter.

TROUBLE IN DODGE

Flora Bella is sick. Three kids down and three to go.

Maybe if I got sick—really good and sick—I could dodge Miss Garr in her relentless hunt for Dr. Love.

"Is it flu?"

"It's the dreaded lurg," says Mum. She is crashing pots around and spilling things. "Dad isn't coming home."

I feel faint. I lean on the counter. "He left?"

"Just for the night, Rex. A business trip."

"Where is he?"

"In Hawkesbury."

"Why?" I ask.

Upstairs, the Sausage starts to cry. I follow Mum down the front hall.

"Because there's a bridge there," she says, turning up the stairs. "Or a water purification plant or something. How should I know?" The baby howls. "Coming, darling!" she shouts.

I follow her into the Sausage's room.

"There, there," she says to my little brother. He looks about as sad as a bowl of yesterday's Cheerios, but he smiles when he sees me and reaches out to touch me. I hold his hand while Mum pours some icky-looking syrup into a spoon.

"It's just as well your father's away," she says. "One less baby to look after."

"But he is coming home, right?"

She feeds the Sausage his medicine and then wipes what he didn't swallow off his chin. Then she lays him gently back down.

"He *is* coming home?"

"What? Oh, give it a break, Rex. Of course he is." She covers the Sausage and gives him his teddy bear, then fixes me with a stare. "Go and be useful," she says. "Entertain your sister."

"Which one?"

"I don't care."

Flora Bella has a thermometer in her mouth. "Can you read this?" she asks. We try to read her temperature. "Two hundred and thirty," she says, and flops back on her pillows.

I give her a hug, hoping lots of germs will leap onto my body. Then I go to visit Annie Oakley.

She is sitting up in bed shooting suction-cup arrows at a target on her closet door.

Thwot!

The arrow sticks onto the wall just above her dresser,

which is where the other two arrows are. Her aim is way off. She throws the bow on the floor and sinks back into her covers.

"Daddy's gone," I say.

She pounds her pillow into shape. "Where is he? In Germany visiting his girlfriend?"

"Stop it, Annie!"

"Maybe it's Erik's birthday."

I want to scream, but I turn to leave.

"Stay," she says, as if I were a dog.

I turn at the door. "Why do you hate him so much?"

She looks miserable. "I don't hate him. I hate liars and cheats."

"You don't know he's a liar and a cheat. You don't know anything." I look down the hall, afraid Mum might hear us. Then I go back to Annie's bedside. "It's just a picture," I say.

"But that boy, Rex. I have this feeling I know him."

"You said that before. Just stop. Okay?"

She doesn't say anything right away. Then, when she speaks, her voice is soft and kind of eerie. "Rex, what if Erik is our *brother*?"

◎ ◎ ◎

James phones that evening. "How was your date?" he asks.

I blush. Luckily he can't see me. I tell him what happened with Natasha.

"Did Larry give her the fat lip?"

"It isn't a fat lip, it's a cleft lip. She was born that way."

"Still," says James. "He's dangerous, isn't he? He gave her a shiner."

"I know."

"So what's going to happen Friday when they have their talk?"

I'm sitting in my father's study, wrapping the phone cord around and around my wrist.

"Rex?"

"I don't know, I don't know, I don't know."

I'm still thinking about what Annie said. I haven't mentioned any of this to my friends—not even James. It's too private, too scary. So we talk about Dr. Love and the letter and what it will be like when the cops come to take us away.

"*Me* away," I remind him.

"Well, I've been thinking about it," he says. "You shouldn't have to go it alone. And it might be fun serving time," he says. "We could smoke and make fake guns out of soap and shoe polish and then make a break for Mexico."

I tell him about my plan to get really sick—at least until Christmas.

"Maybe I should come over and catch the dreaded lurg, too," he says.

I hang up the phone and sit for a long time in my father's tippy chair, soaking up the quiet of the study. I can hear Letitia singing in the kitchen as she does the dishes.

I reach for the phone. I know the number by heart. I dial and hold my breath.

"Natasha?"

"Hello, Rex. How are you?"

I swallow. This is only the second time in my life I've talked to a girl on the phone. "I wanted to thank you for the ice cream."

"It was my pleasure," she says, but I interrupt her because I need to say what's on my mind.

"And I'm worried about Friday."

She pauses. The line crackles. I can hear music in the background. Jazz.

"I don't think that's anything you need to worry about," she says at last. She doesn't sound very convincing. I'm about to say something about him hitting her again, but she starts talking and her voice is different now, almost happy.

"We used to talk all the time," she says. "He would get home after a long road trip and tell me about some funny thing that happened in a truck stop in Oromocto, or how crazy the warehouse manager was at some factory in Peru. Peru, Indiana, if there is such a place. I swear sometimes he made things up, but it was funny." She chuckles. "He could do voices . . . you know, impersonate people. He'd have me laughing."

The line goes silent again.

"That's the kind of talk I'm hoping for," she says, after a while. "He'll walk in that door at seven o'clock and I'll have some tasty casserole ready and it will be just like old times." Her voice wavers a bit as she finishes.

I clear my throat. "I hope so, too, Natasha."

"Anyway, I appreciate your concern. Don't worry. You hear me?"

"Okay," I say.

But when I hang up I am worried.

◎ ◎ ◎

I watch *Gunsmoke* with Mum. Everyone else has gone to bed. It's *way* past my bedtime, but she doesn't say anything and I think maybe she's lonely.

Marshal Dillon is the law in Dodge City. He's talking to Miss Kitty, who runs the saloon. I have only seen the show a couple of times, but I know that she is his special friend. You can tell by the way she takes off his hat when he steps up to the bar. There's trouble in town. There's always trouble.

She pours him a drink. When he's finished, he puts the glass down on the bar and grabs his hat. "Sometimes, a man's got to do . . ." he says.

". . . what a man's got to do." She finishes the sentence for him. They chuckle together. I guess he's said that more than once. It's what Dad said to me when he didn't want to talk about the war.

That night I lie in bed thinking about all the things a man's got to do. I hope, like Marshal Dillon, I will always know what to do. And when to do it.

... WHAT A MAN'S GOT TO DO

Buster is back! He is there waiting in the school yard before the bell, and he comes right up as soon as I walk through the gate.

"I didn't mean what I said," he says. "I was just kind of . . . scared, I guess."

"Me, too."

"But I'm ready now."

I nod. Can't speak. Nod some more.

Buster scratches his flattop. He looks puzzled. "What is it we're going to do?"

I shrug. "Don't know."

"Okay," he says. "I can do that."

But as soon as Miss Garr takes attendance, I know. And I'm going to do it alone.

Donnie is still away and she smiles a crocodile smile.

"Well, children. That empty chair by the window speaks volumes, doesn't it?"

Everybody looks around as if we're not sure what she means.

"Oh, surely you understand plain English," says Miss Garr. "This is the second day in a row that Donald has been away. I have checked with the office and there has been no call from his parents."

Kathy puts up her hand. "Maybe they moved?"

"I doubt it," says Miss Garr. "But we will soon find out. A truant officer from the school board will be calling on the Dangerfields today. I am sure that Donald is playing hooky. Ducking his responsibility."

Sami leans forward and whispers in my ear. "Donald Ducking," he says. And I snort—I can't help myself.

"Rex? Is something the matter?"

"No, ma'am," I say. Then I realize that Sami has just given me my chance to do something. "Actually, yes, Miss Garr. There is something I want to say."

"Fine. Stand, please. I don't need to ask you to speak up, do I, because you always speak so clearly. Go ahead."

I stand up. I only wish I had a hat like Marshal Dillon's. "Ma'am, about that letter. Donnie didn't send it to you."

Miss Garr looks confused, as if I accidentally started talking in Martian. I can feel my classmates looking at me and I know I'd better hurry before the wobbly feeling in my legs gets any worse.

"I did," I say. "And I'm really sorry."

There is a big intake of breath, as if the class sucked up

every ounce of air. I feel myself growing faint. I put one hand on my desk for support.

Miss Garr looks at the floor. I can almost see the rocks there in front of her. See her choosing a big pointy one to throw at me.

"Don't be ridiculous, Rex," she says with a weary sigh.

"It's true. Donnie didn't send it. I did."

She tilts her head my way and sizes me up.

"I'm sure you think this is noble," she says. "Shielding Donald Dangerfield."

"No, ma'am. It's true."

Then there is a noise behind me. It's Zoltan Kádár getting to his feet.

"He is lying," says Zoltan. "I sent letter."

Miss Garr's mouth drops. Then she snaps it shut. "Nonsense," she says. "With all due respect, Mr. Kádár, you can barely string together a sentence, let alone a whole letter."

Zoltan just smiles.

"I get help," he says.

Then Kathy Brown stands up. "Zoltan is only saying that because he doesn't want you to find out the truth."

"Really?" says Miss Garr. "Which is?"

"*I* sent the letter."

Now everyone laughs.

"That's not true," says Polly, jumping up. "It was me."

Then, behind me, Sami jumps up.

"It was me, Miss Garr. I wrote the letter."

And the class goes wild.

"Enough!" shouts Miss Garr. She is turning bright red. Fire engine red. "This is monstrous!" She claps her hands. "Stop it immediately!"

The laughter slowly dies and the teacher glares at me, Kathy, Sami, Zoltan, and finally Polly. "I would have expected more from you, Miss Goldstein, in your position as class president. Sit down. All of you."

One by one the others sit until there is just Kathy and me.

"Miss Brown? Did you hear me?"

"Yes, ma'am." But Kathy doesn't sit. So I guess I'm not alone, after all.

Miss Garr glares at Kathy, but can't get her to sit, so she shifts her attention to me. "Have you got waxy buildup in your ears, Mr. Norton-Norton?"

"No, ma'am. I'm only trying to tell you that I was the one who sent you the letter. Really. I'm sorry I didn't tell you yesterday. I was too afraid."

I try to hold Miss Garr's gaze, but it is too frightening. Her shoulders are stiff. Her whole body is rigid. Buster was right; she looks like the Bride of Frankenstein.

"We were in it together," says Kathy. Her voice is quiet but determined. Just looking at her makes me feel braver.

"All right," says Miss Garr. "If that's the way you two want it."

"It isn't the way we want it," I say. "It's just true. And it was mostly my fault. I wish I'd never done it. It wasn't meant to hurt you."

Her mouth opens in disbelief. "Good God! What was it meant to do, then? Answer me that."

I look down. I wish the police would come and take me to prison. I'd go quietly. Anything to get out of this room!

"I asked you a question!" she shrieks.

I look at her. "I can explain," I say. "But not here. In the office?"

I can hardly believe I said that. But right now, seeing the principal actually seems like a good idea.

"Get up here," she says. "This instant!"

There is a noise from the back of the class. Zoltan is getting out of his seat.

"Sit down!" she shouts at him, but he won't. He walks up the aisle and reaches the front at the same time as I do. Then Kathy comes, too, and all Miss Garr can do is back away, in shock, until she is leaning against the blackboard. Now Polly is on her feet and joins us.

"Whatever you do to him, you do to me," says Zoltan.

"And me," says Kathy.

"And me," says Polly.

Miss Garr's hands grasp the blackboard tray and her knuckles are as white as chalk. But her face is red and writhing like a bag full of snakes.

"You will all be suspended," she says in a voice drained

of energy, as if she has little breath left. "You will all be punished for this, severely. Do. You. Understand?"

I look at the others. We all nod.

She catches her breath, stands up straight. Squares her shoulders. She walks to her desk and opens the bottom drawer. I feel Polly tense beside me. I grab hold of her hand and she squeezes it tight.

Miss Garr leans heavily on her desktop and doesn't move for a moment. Then she takes another deep breath and pulls out the strap.

From up close, the strap looks thicker, more lethal. Worst of all, clutching it seems to give Miss Garr renewed strength, though she doesn't look at all well.

"I thought you were different from the others, Rex," she says. "I thought you were polite and well behaved, respectful. I see that I was wrong. Put out your hand."

I let go of Polly's hand and step forward. Slowly, shakily, I hold out my hand.

I look into Miss Garr's eyes. They are glassy. There are tears there.

I feel almost sorry for her. She looks like someone caught in a nightmare and the only escape is to thrash her way out with this thick green strap.

She raises her hand to shoulder height.

"Don't," says Polly.

"Quiet!" shouts Miss Garr.

And then, suddenly, the door at the back of the class-room opens. Everyone turns to look.

It's Donnie. Donnie Dangerfield. His arm is in a sling. He's wearing a cast. He looks at us standing in the front and a wide grin cracks his face in half.

"Wow!" he says. "What did I miss?"

Then there is a terrible choking, wheezing sound. It's Miss Garr. She drops the belt and her hand flies to her chest. And before anyone can move, she collapses.

. . . AND GOT TO DO

The ambulance comes and takes Miss Garr away. Then Mr. Johnstone, the principal, comes into the classroom and we tell him everything. Not just what happened today, but everything stretching back to the very first day she arrived.

He listens—really listens. At one point he looks at Donnie's broken arm as if maybe Miss Garr did that, too.

"I ran into a brick wall," says Donnie. We all laugh, even Mr. Johnstone. It's good to laugh.

The Dr. Love letter is in Miss Garr's top drawer. Mr. Johnstone takes it and reads it in his office at his desk. Kathy, James, and Buster are here with me, waiting. At one point he stops reading and picks up a pencil to circle something. He circles a bunch of things. He's marking it!

"I'm sure you realize there will be repercussions," he says when he's done. I'm not exactly sure what a repercussion is or how many of them he has in mind, but I'm pretty sure we're not looking at a stretch in the penitentiary.

"Will we get the strap?" asks Buster. He's already hiding his hands in his armpits.

Mr. Johnstone looks very serious, but he shakes his head. "There won't be any more strapping in this school," he says. "That's a form of punishment from another era, one I find particularly disagreeable."

We are all relieved. We must look too relieved, I guess.

"I'm not finished," says Mr. Johnstone. "I will think good and hard about what you have done and I expect you to do the same. There will be ramifications."

I'm not sure if a ramification is better or worse than a repercussion. I'm hoping he will explain exactly what he has in mind, but he stares at the letter again, and looks pretty gloomy.

"I'll tell you one thing," he says. "You're all going to have extra spelling homework."

Kathy's mother is the first one to arrive. Then James's mother comes and takes him away, and Buster's, last of all. My mum can't come on account of the dreaded lurg. So I sit outside the office the whole day and then I'm allowed to walk home on my own.

Someone calls me as I'm leaving the playground.

It's Sandy Ermanovics. "Hear you killed Miss Garr," he says excitedly.

"She had a heart attack," I tell him. "The hospital called

the office and she's in stable condition." He looks disappointed.

"I forgot to tell you," he says. "Some guy at my dad's office lost his address book. If you want, my dad could give it back to him."

"Thanks," I say. I'm too tired to explain that the mystery has already been solved. I'll tell him tomorrow. But as I'm walking away, something occurs to me and I call out to Sandy.

"Could you get the guy's phone number from your father?"

"Sure," he says. Sandy's really friendly all of a sudden, as if there's nothing he wouldn't do for me. "I'll call you later, okay?"

I nod and head off toward my doom. Even though it's already getting dark, I know the day is a long way from over.

"Oh my," says Mum. "A heart attack? The poor woman."

I keep my lips buttoned.

"How could you do such a thing, Rex?"

This feels like one of those times when you need to stick to the facts and not try to get around things or blame anybody else. Besides, I'm kind of worn out. I just want to lie down.

"It was a mistake," I say.

"I'll say," says Mum. Upstairs the Sausage is wailing. "Wait in your father's study," she says. "He can deal with you."

And so I don't get to go to my room and lie down. I wait. A man's got to do what a man's got to do, got to do, got to do, got to do!

It looks like being a man is going to be a full-time job.

I sit in the tilty chair behind the desk and put my feet up. But I'm not Sam Spade anymore, just really, really tired.

Suddenly, my eyes snap open. I'm staring at the top row of the bookshelf, where Dad keeps his history books. I look at the thick volume bound in red with gold relief, and remember the time I walked into the study and he was putting that book away, standing on a footstool. He looked all red in the face. I remember thinking it was the strain of reaching so high.

I grab hold of the desk and sit upright. Then I look again at the red book. It almost seems as if there is a red light inside it flashing on and off.

The secret cache!

I look at the clock. Four-thirty. Dad is never home before five. I've got time if I hurry. But how am I going to get to it?

I try the footstool. It doesn't help much. I place my right foot on the edge of the second shelf. I pull myself up. I teeter a bit but manage to get my balance. I catch my breath and reach my foot up to the next shelf. It takes all my strength to pull myself up.

I glance down. I'm only about three feet off the ground, but I feel as dizzy as if I were on the side of Mount Everest!

I look up. The book is still the full length of my arm above my head. Squashing my face against the book spines, I stand on my tiptoes, reaching as high as I can with my left hand.

I find it—grab it. The book is as thick as a dictionary. I look up again to make sure I have the right one. Yes.

But there is a problem. I'm all twisted around. I should have started climbing with my left foot, but it's too late to try to turn around now. Slowly, slowly I pull the book out, leaning back a little. I brace myself. It slides out easily enough, but I doubt I'll be able to hold it with only one hand once it's free of the shelf. I rest before pulling it the last bit. My nose is itchy, full of book dust and mildew. If worst comes to worst, I can drop the book and hope it doesn't make too much noise on the carpet.

Then I realize that if I can direct it toward the wingback chair—sort of throw it—the book will have an even softer landing.

I take a deep breath, hold on tight, and pull the book all the way out.

Which is when the door opens behind me.

And my foot slips.

And the book flies from my hands.

And I start to fall.

"Rex!"

THE TIGHTROPE

’m amazed at how long it takes to hit the floor. I was only about three feet up, after all, and yet I keep falling and falling. And papers are flying everywhere around me. Pictures and postcards and letters written on thin blue paper whirling and fluttering like birds set free.

"Ow!"

I open my eyes. The walls are slanted above me. I'm not in the study anymore. I'm in bed. Mum is wrapping a bandage tightly around my wrist.

"Well, well, well," she says. "Sir Edmund Hillary, back from the brink."

I look at my wing—my arm. It feels like a bunch of squirrels are having a nut-throwing party inside it.

"Is it broken?"

Mum clears up her things from beside her on the bed. "I shouldn't think so. But you won't be writing any Dr. Love letters for a while."

Then it all comes back to me. Why couldn't I have just kept falling?

"Dr. McFarlane will be here a little later," says Mum. She stands up and looks down at me sternly. I think I catch the glimmer of a tiny smile, but maybe that's just wishful thinking. Then she turns toward the far end of the room.

"The prisoner is all yours," she says.

Dad. He's leaning against my desk.

Mum leaves without another word, pulling the door shut behind her. I half expect to hear a key turn, locking us in.

My father's arms are folded on his chest. The sleeves of his white shirt are rolled up like he means business. His face is grim. His eyes . . . I can't even find his eyes. They are lost in the shadows cast by the granite overhang of his forehead.

I must have a fever. I lay my head back on my pillow.

"Let's see if I've got this right," he says. "You were waiting in my study to hear your punishment for sticking your nose into other people's business, and while there, you thought, why don't I just scale this bookcase and see if there's any personal business *here* I can stick my nose into?"

I swallow. My throat feels parched. Glancing at my bedside table, I see a glass of water, but I'm not sure if I dare to reach for it.

"Well?" he says.

"Yes, sir."

He doesn't say anything for such a long time I strain my

neck again to see if he is still there. He hasn't moved a muscle. His pipe is sticking out of his breast pocket. Why isn't he fiddling around with his pipe? At least then I'd know he was really my father.

"This letter sounds like a pretty idiotic idea," he says.

I nod, which is hard to do when your head is lying on a pillow.

"Dr. *Love*?"

Coming from him it sounds completely stupid. It is stupid! But somehow I can tell it isn't Dr. Love he's cross about.

If only he'd come closer so that I could see his eyes.

Suddenly I wonder if he'll ever come close to me again. I wonder if I've driven him away forever. I wonder if he'll ever want me to go with him anywhere. I want to say that I would go with him to a hundred Armistice Day ceremonies in a row if he'd only give me another chance.

"What are we going to do with you?" he says.

I don't have any idea.

"Is nothing sacred?"

No idea at all.

"Are the only secrets the ones that *you* keep, Rex?"

We're edging closer to it.

"No, sir."

"Good. Then you'll admit it's possible that someone—even a parent—might have a perfectly good reason to keep something from you?"

"Yes, sir."

"What's that?"

He can't hear me because the words barely make it out of my mouth. I swallow and my throat hurts. I point at the glass of water. Finally, he comes to me. I try to prop myself up, forgetting about my wrist. I cry out in pain. He helps me up, fixes my pillows, hands me the glass. Then, while I drink, he gets the chair from my desk and brings it over to my bed. I hand him the empty glass.

"I'm sorry, Daddy."

"I know," he says. But he's still peeved. He sighs. "I also know that you weren't operating alone."

I cradle my sore wrist in my arms and stare at him.

"I had a chance to talk with your accomplice."

"Annie?"

"She's in leg irons in the basement," he says. Then he reaches for his pipe. "I'm working on a deal to sell her to the Mau Maus to use as hippopotamus bait."

"She found this picture—"

"So I hear. And she wondered if Erik was a long-lost half brother."

"But he isn't, is he? I mean she felt like she knew him and that made her think that he must be a relative or . . . well, you know."

"Yes, I do know," he says wearily. "I understand, Rex. And no, Erik is not my son. There, are you happy?"

I nod. But I'm not happy, really. It still doesn't explain who the pretty woman is, who the letters are from, why he keeps them hidden. And anyway, my father's not happy, so how can I be?

Meanwhile, he has found his little pipe-cleaning gizmo and starts reaming out the bowl.

"Your sister felt she knew Erik for the simple reason that she *has* met him before."

I can hardly believe my ears. "She *met* him?"

Dad nods without looking up. "I suppose I'll have no rest until I explain," he says. And then, without lighting his pipe, he does.

"The woman in the picture is named Inge," he says. "Inge Eckhart. She was a war widow when I met her, with a baby son and not much else."

"Erik."

"Yes, Erik."

Then Dad tells me the story of how he helped Inge and her son find shelter, food, warm clothing. Everything was chaos in the cities—as bad in Germany as everywhere else. He spoke a little German—more German than she spoke English. He helped her with the authorities. She had lost her husband, her home—everything.

He sighs. "Some of the men were too embittered to lend a hand. Couldn't do it. They were filled with rage. And I understood it, Rex. So was I. You can have no idea. We had seen comrades die, our own cities back home bombed mercilessly. And yet . . . and yet helping Inge . . . well, it was a jolly sight better than shooting people."

He leans on his knees and looks down at the carpet. It's a bit threadbare, but my father looks as if he is trying to weave the color back into it again with his eyes.

"Do you know what the best thing in the world is, Rex?"

"No, sir."

"To be useful." He grins. "Oh," he says, "that will sound as dull as dishwater to a young spark like you. But, believe me, being useful—helping out—seemed like a bloody great gift after what we'd been through."

He isn't looking at me now, and he's given up on the carpet. He's looking through a hole in the air back to another time somewhere. He's told me something about those times: laying down a length of bridge through the mud to keep the troops moving; digging a bunker; sneaking up on a sniper. And now, I guess, he's finding clothing for a widow and her little boy.

"So, she became your friend?" I ask.

He nods. "Helped me to work through the anger," he says. "Helped me to feel . . . what . . . human again. Can you understand that?"

He turns his gaze on me and I have never seen such a look in his eyes. A few moments earlier I was afraid I had lost him—that he would never trust me again. Now I realize that he is entrusting me with something huge, and I'm not sure I'm up to it.

Mein Liebchen, she called him. That sounds like more than a friend.

He holds me with his eyes. It's as if we have stepped onto a tightrope stretching across a chasm. He has a firm grip on me, but I still might fall if I look down. I have to stare into his eyes and believe in him, or this rope will snap.

I wonder if he can see what is in my eyes—what *I* want with all my heart. I want him to say what Natasha said to me about Mr. Dance. I want my father to tell me that he and Inge were *just* friends. Can't he see that? I feel as if he can.

So why won't he say it? He only has to say it with his eyes—that's all I'm asking.

My eyes plead with him. But he will not give me what I want. He wants only to get me across the abyss. He holds me steady in his gaze, and now all I want is my father back! The funny one who can't be serious about anything for long. I want him to say something silly, tell me a tall tale, spin me a yarn.

I don't want him to tell me this.

My wrist aches. My whole body aches. It's worse than when Miss Garr was going to give me the strap. Getting the strap would have been *easy* compared to this.

Why?

And right away, I know why. *Because I don't love Miss Garr and nothing she could do could hurt me this much.*

And suddenly we're there on the other side, together, my father and I. We made it. I'm wobbly. It will take a long time to recover, but we made it!

From his other breast pocket Dad fishes out the picture of Erik and his mother leaning against the front of a car.

"This is when they came to visit us in England," he says. "She had remarried by then. A bloke named Peter. Good chap. That's my Austin they're leaning against. I've told you about my Austin, haven't I?"

"The one you ran over the cat with?"

"The very same. Horrible cat."

I take the picture from him and hold it with both hands. It's as if we just stepped off that tightrope and this photograph is the first piece of solid land. I want to hold on to it as tightly as I can.

"No wonder Annie thought she recognized Erik," he says. "She was just a little tyke, but she fell in love with him. 'What's the nine-year-old doing now?' she'd ask. Or, 'Can the nine-year-old come out and play?' She never called him Erik—always the nine-year-old."

"Where's Mum?" I ask.

"Probably with the children."

"No, I mean in the picture."

He smiles. "Probably with the children," he says.

"And Inge's husband?"

"He was probably playing the piano. He was quite a pianist. Wait a second."

Dad reaches out, takes the photograph from me, and holds it to his ear. "Yes," he says. "If you listen very closely you can just hear it. Some awful Strauss waltz, I think, but rather jolly."

So I take the photograph and hold it close to me and listen for all I'm worth. And I can almost hear it. The music.

STONES

When I get a chance I ask Mum if it was Inge she wanted Dad to tell me about.

"Good gracious no," she says. "Inge wasn't the problem." Mum is kneading bread. She gives it a good hard punch. "Sorted him out, she did."

I'm not sure what she means, but from the way she's going at the bread dough I figure it best not to go on about Inge anymore.

She sighs and goes back to kneading. But I can see she's thinking and I wait patiently, leaning on the counter.

She pushes her hair off her face with her wrist. She gets a flour smudge on her forehead, but I don't say anything.

"There were *other* things that happened in the war," she says. "Things that are like stones on your father's heart."

It's such a strange thing for her to say that I'm struck dumb.

She rolls the dough over and sprinkles it with flour. She's about to knead it again, but she pauses.

"Toward the end of the war . . ."

She stops as if already she's gone too far. I hold my breath.

"They'd heard rumors, of course," she says, as if I already know what she's talking about.

"Rumors about what?"

"Horrible things," she says. "Atrocities." Her face is hard, every muscle tense. Then she shakes her head. "Oh, it's not for me to say, Rex."

Atrocities. I know about atrocities.

"The camps?"

She looks at me solemnly.

"The . . . concentration camps?"

After a moment, she nods. I sit down hard on the nearest chair.

"Bergen-Belsen," she says. She looks out the window. A gust of wind blows the snow into a whirlwind and the garden disappears. "British and Canadian troops liberated Bergen-Belsen in 1945. April 15, 1945."

For a moment I'm dazzled, thinking of the troops liberating the camp. Was Dad one of them? He must have been. That's why Mum remembers the exact date. He must have been so happy and proud helping to set free all those prisoners.

I look at Mum and her face is stony silent. Gray. She's

not one bit happy. She's watching me, waiting. Making me think for myself.

And now a movie reel starts clicking in my head. A war documentary I must have seen on television. Photographs of concentration camps. I stare at Mum and she reads my mind. Her voice, when she speaks, is extra soft.

"He was an engineer, Rex. Someone had to clean the place up."

It's utterly quiet except for the wind in the garden. Then I hear my mother swallow.

I look at her. She looks worried. I try to let her know I'm okay. I can handle it. I don't want to let her down.

Do you know what the best thing in the world is, Rex? To be useful.

Then I remember something else my father said to me a million years ago when I was pestering him about the stuff my sisters didn't know—stuff that was not for delicate ears. *I'm not sure that now's the time,* he said. Suddenly I know what he meant.

It isn't time. I'm not ready.

And yet . . . I want to help. I want to be useful.

I stare at my mother kneading, kneading. She glances my way.

"What do I do?"

She stops. Shrugs.

"I don't know, Rex," she says. "He has nightmares. Even now. I thought he should talk to someone. But he won't see a doctor. You know what he's like. And he won't go down to the Legion—talk to other old soldiers." She pushes the dough around. "I wasn't sure who to turn to. Then when he asked you to go to the service at the War Memorial . . ."

She looks at me with this hopeful look.

Has she forgotten what happened on Armistice Day? No, I don't think so. Dad wanted me to go with him. That's the point. Sure I blew it, but this is my chance to make up for it.

"Should I ask him about it?"

She smiles at last and rolls her eyes. "Rex, I think your father has had quite enough of you for the time being."

"I know. But sometime—some other time?"

"Yes," she says. "That would be good." She takes a knife, cuts off a section of the dough, and plops it in a bread pan. I carry it to the hearth in the living room where it's warm and the dough can rise. I wait and take the next and the next. Six loaves rising.

"Many hands make light work," she says. It's something she says a lot, especially when she wants us to help clean up. I take a tea towel and wipe the flour smudge off her forehead.

MANY HANDS MAKE LIGHT WORK

Many hands make light work. That's what I think about as Friday approaches. There are a lot of things to think about, but right now, there is one last battle to fight, the battle of Friday night. The battle of the Lavenders.

Natasha Lavender. I see her in my mind's eye the way I saw her that first time, standing at the window of twenty-nine Quigley Street, staring out at the darkness, looking so sad.

Then I see her saying goodbye to Larry. Hear how mean he is. See the black eye he left her with as a going-away present.

I see her in the Two-by-Four, the time when I warned her and Mr. Dance that Larry was on his way. I see the fear in her face.

Then I see her the other time at the Two-by-Four, when she tried so hard to explain what had happened between her and Mr. Dance and between her and Larry.

Last of all, I hear her telling me on the phone about how much fun Larry used to be and how she hopes when he gets back he'll have a story or two to tell her. If he doesn't— if he's mean and miserable—then they'll have to have a good long talk. That's what she said.

And that's what worries me.

I phone Wilfred Dance. He's worried about Natasha, too, but he can't go over.

"If she asked me, I'd be there in a shot," he says. "But I shouldn't interfere. It would make matters worse. You can see that, can't you, Rex?"

I guess I can. My own interfering has already got me into big trouble. I'm not sure I want to poke my nose into any other people's business. But then I remember what Dad said. How the best thing was to be useful. What am I supposed to do?

Then I get a sign.

Wednesday night. *The Magnificent Seven* is on TV—the best cowboy movie of all. These hired gunmen root out the bandits who are devastating a helpless Mexican town. They work together and nothing can stop them.

"Larry sounds mean and sneaky like a bandit," says James, when I tell him my plan the next day.

"So is Natasha the helpless Mexican town?" asks Buster.

"Kind of."

There are even seven of us, just like in the movie: James, Buster, Sami, Kathy, Donnie, Zoltan, and me. Donnie's got a broken arm and I've got a sprained wrist, but who cares?

"What is plan?" asks Zoltan.

"We listen," I say.

"That's all? Listen?"

I nod. I tell them about the entranceway at number twenty-nine, how there's room for all of us as long we're quiet, so we don't have to stand outside in the cold.

"And you can hear good?" says Zoltan.

"If he starts yelling or throwing stuff, we'll hear it, all right."

"If he does start throwing stuff, what then?" says Donnie. He looks excited, as if throwing stuff is right up his alley.

"We'll knock on the door," says James.

"Boring," says Buster. "How 'bout I bring my bowie knife?"

"No way!"

"We'll keep knocking until he comes down," says Kathy. "And?"

"And we'll tell him we'll call the police."

"We should at least take a baseball bat or something," says Donnie.

"We don't need weapons," I say. "There are seven of us."

It snows again on Friday from early in the morning until late afternoon. It's beautiful. By evening, the clouds have scudded away and the moon has come out. Perfect.

We trudge over to Quigley Street in high spirits as if we're going bowling or to a movie. It's hard to think things might get dangerous. But as we approach the apartment building, the butterflies inside me wake up and start doing the Watusi in my stomach.

The lights are on. It's seven-fifteen. We stamp the snow off our feet outside on the front porch and then head inside.

"Shhhhhhh!"

But we aren't anywhere near quiet enough. Seven people in a small entranceway is as good as a herd. In no time the door to apartment 1A opens and a tiny old lady with her hair up in curlers peers out at us.

"Carolers!" she cries, clapping her hands together. "What are you going to sing?"

We look around at each other. Then Donnie starts "Speed Bonnie Boat." I join in, but the old woman in apartment 1A is not amused.

"That's no Christmas carol," she says.

"That's because it isn't Christmas," says James.

That's when the door to apartment 1B opens and a fat man with suspenders over a stained T-shirt peers out at us.

"What is this?" he says, rubbing his belly.

"Uh, we're just visiting," says Kathy.

"Visiting who?" says the fat man. "There ain't no kids in this place."

"My aunt," I say. And I point at the door to 2B.

The man doesn't look convinced. But James steps forward. "Sorry, Mr. Derouin," he says. "We didn't mean to make so much noise. But our aunt doesn't seem to be home yet."

The man looks suspiciously at James and then back at me. "She's your aunt, too?"

"She is all our aunt," says Zoltan.

The man makes a sour face, shakes his head, and closes the door.

"How'd you know his name?" I whisper.

"The mailbox," says James.

"Shhhh!" says Sami. "Listen."

Sure enough, we hear raised voices. Buster puts his ear up against the door to 2B and his eyes grow wide.

"It's them, all right."

"Or it's him, anyway," says James.

I take a turn at the door. Larry is hot about something.

"What's he saying?" says Sami.

"Try door," says Zoltan. He reaches through the crowd and slowly turns the knob.

To our surprise it is unlocked. He pulls it open just a crack. Now we can hear everything.

"Don't tell me you weren't seeing him."

"For a coffee, Larry. We're friends."

"Friends, my foot. Why I oughta . . ."

"*No*, Larry," says Natasha, raising her voice. "You ought *not* to!"

"Don't you *ever* tell *me* what I can or can't *do*!" he says.

Then there is a loud smack and a cry.

All of us start pounding on the door and stamping our feet and shouting up the stairs. In no time 1A and 1B are out in the entranceway again, yelling at us and threatening to call the cops.

"Good idea," says Zoltan.

Then we hear footsteps coming from above and everyone goes quiet and steps back. Larry comes down the staircase, tucking in his shirt.

"What the . . ."

"These kids," says 1B. "They friends of yours?"

"Are you kiddin' me?" says Larry. He looks us over. "You think I hang out with the seven dwarfs?"

"I'm not dwarf," says Zoltan, stepping toward Larry. He's almost exactly Larry's height and he's not afraid of him, either. Larry steps backward onto the first step of the staircase to make himself taller.

"What is all this rumpus?" says old Mrs. 1A.

Kathy points at Larry. "He was beating up his wife," she says.

"Whoa, whoa, whoa!" says Larry. "What'd you say?"

"You heard her," says Donnie.

"You hit her," I say.

Larry looks at me with my bandaged wrist and at Donnie with his arm in a sling and at Kathy. It's as if he's considering the odds. He smirks. Then Zoltan presses closer, his fists at the ready. And the smirk vanishes from Larry's face.

"Get the hell out of here," he says. "The lot of you."

"No," I say.

"You're the one who should get out of here," says Kathy.

1B grins. "Looks like they got you outnumbered, Larry," he says.

"Shut up, fatso." Larry raises his fist and shakes it at his neighbor, who backs toward his door. Then Larry turns to us and holds up a finger. "I gonna count to five," he says.

"Wow!" says Donnie. "So high?"

Larry's eyes go all squinty, as if he just stepped into some episode of *The Twilight Zone* and nothing makes sense anymore. He takes another step back up the stairs.

"I didn't touch her, okay."

"Yes, you did."

It's Natasha. She's standing at the top of the staircase. Now she comes down slowly, holding the railing tightly. She's wearing a red cocktail dress. Her cheek is red, too.

"Yes, you did, Larry," she says again. "And it's the last time you'll ever hit me."

"Hey," he says. "Come on, hon. It was just a little tap."

That's when old Mrs. 1A barges her way through the bunch of us and pokes Larry in the chest.

"Little tap, my Aunt Fanny!" she says. "You think I don't hear what goes on up there?"

"Ah, can it," says Larry.

But Mrs. 1A taps him in the chest again so hard he winces. By then, Natasha is standing right behind him. I notice she's carrying his plaid jacket, a scarf, gloves, and a pair of boots.

"Here," she says. Then she shoves the clothes at Larry so hard, she knocks him off his step. "I tried, Larry. I really tried. But it's no use. So just go."

Larry pulls himself up tall. He rubs his nose. "Yeah, well, maybe a little air would be good," he says. "It sure stinks around here."

He shoves us aside and heads toward the door. He stops and pats his pockets. "My wallet," he says.

"It's in your coat."

"And my house key?"

Natasha shakes her head. "Call me," she says. "We'll arrange a time for you to come and get your things."

"You can't do this to me," says Larry. He looks furious.

"You want me to get the lease?" she says. "It's only got my name on it, Larry."

The fury drains out of him like dirty water from a sink. He's standing right in the middle of us and he doesn't look scary at all anymore.

"Ah, Larry," says Natasha sadly, almost affectionately.

"You're not so tough when you've got a crowd of witnesses, are you?"

He peers at us one by one, as if he's memorizing our faces. He's trying so hard to look tough. Kathy is standing by the front door. She opens it and cold air pours in. She taps him on the shoulder.

His eyes fly to her hand as if maybe she's got a weapon or something. Then he brushes his shoulder where she tapped him. He looks at her—at all of us—a little sorrowfully. And, as crazy as it sounds, I can almost see why Natasha liked him once upon a time.

Then he's gone.

I don't know what I'm expecting. I turn to Natasha as if maybe she'll invite us all up for a Coke. But she's crying. And so we leave. Just like that.

We head over to Buster's and get there in time for *Shock Theatre.* It's *Plan 9 from Outer Space* and we laugh ourselves silly.

I walk home, alone but happy, through the thick snow.

This snow isn't going to melt. Not soon, anyway. This is the real thing.

EPILOGUE

iss Garr doesn't come back. After Christmas she starts teaching grade one at another school and is very happy. Our new teacher tells us all about it. She wonders if we would like to send Miss Garr a card or flowers or chocolates or something. We send a card.

Kathy's mom marries Dr. Arnold Schwartz right before Christmas and then all four of them go away together on the honeymoon. When they get back, they move into Dr. Arnold's big house. It takes Kathy some getting used to. We help out by coming over to eat pizza and watch TV. Missy feels like she got herself a whole big family!

And that's not all. Cassiopeia is engaged to Mr. Odsburg. She can't stop looking at her diamond ring. I ask him if he got it for free because he works in precious jewels. He says no, but he got a good price on it. They're going to get married in the summer.

Winter sets in, shiny and cold, and by mid-January the Rideau Canal is safe to skate on.

One Saturday, I'm down there with the gang. They can all skate circles around me because I'm only just learning and they've been skating since they were three days old or something. But I don't care.

Anyway, I'm shuffling along, more on my ankles than anything else, while the others play tag, when suddenly I look up and see Natasha Lavender and Mr. Dance. They're skating arm in arm.

I shout and almost fall down. They skate over. Natasha even does a little twirl. She looks extra specially beautiful with her cheeks all rosy.

It turns out Larry moved west, to Alberta, where there are lots of jobs. He and Natasha are getting a divorce. She doesn't mind waiting, she says, and Mr. Dance gives her a hug.

She kisses me on the cheek and they skate off, turning to wave—twice—before they disappear into the crowd. The kiss feels cool on my cheek. I touch it, except you can't really touch a kiss. It's there and then it's gone.

"Hey, Rex, come on!" It's James. He points toward the stand where they sell hot cinnamon rolls.

I wave and shuffle along to catch up—shaky but learning fast.